ISLAND SECRETS

STORIES OF LOVE, LUST AND LOSS FROM BALI

ALWIN BLUM

monsoon

monsoonbooks

Published in 2017
by Monsoon Books Ltd
www.monsoonbooks.co.uk

No.1 Duke of Windsor Suite, Burrough Court,
Burrough on the Hill, Leicestershire LE14 2QS, UK

ISBN (paperback): 978-1-912049-26-4
ISBN (ebook): 978-1-912049-27-1

Cover design by Cover Kitchen.

Printed in Great Britain by Clays Ltd, St Ives plc
20 19 18 17   1 2 3 4 5

A NOTE ON BALINESE NAMES

Traditionally, most Balinese are named according to their birth order. Namely Wayan, the eldest; Made (pronounced Ma-day) is for the second child; Nyoman, the third-born; Ketut, the fourth child. The names are repeated if there are more than four children, for example, the fifth-born may be named Wayan Balik which means Wayan Again. This is why similar names are found all over Bali for both men and women. While each person has a second or third name, their birth order names like Wayan, Nyoman, etc are the ones everyone uses daily. The Balinese do not have family names. Upper caste families will have names denoting their caste; Agung (or Anak Agung) for instance, is a royal or warrior caste name, or Ida Bagus which is for a man from the Brahmana (Brahmin) or priest caste which is the highest caste. These caste signifiers are usually followed by another two, three, or more personal names.

CONTENTS

A TREMBLING LAND

The first night they spent together the earth shook. They were in bed, sweaty and naked and thirsty. It was their very first time away together after so many long looks across dining tables, their unspoken hunger all balled up in lingering, yearning gazes across crowded rooms. These soon graduated to prolonged touches, an advantage he took as he passed her a glass of wine, his fingers closing over hers when they were safely out of sight of the rest. Or the hand she quietly placed on his arm as she showed him a glossy coffee-table book on Balinese women.

These furtive touches soon turned into stolen embraces with long, deep kisses accompanying feverish groping and kneading of breasts, hips and loins, like two teenagers in heat. She was the respectable foreign wife of a respectable Balinese man. He was a nomadic academic from home who spoke fluent Indonesian in addition to four other Southeast Asian languages, a man thrice married, once engaged and very familiar with these forbidden assignations all around the world.

* * *

The first time Tanya met Ken, he was on holiday with his teaching assistant, Elizabeth. He was obviously growing less enamoured with the pretty young woman who was half his age. He was

civil with the girl but his tone was increasingly curt, even as she clung to his every word – Ken was her mentor and now her lover. Elizabeth had been the perfect excuse for him to get out of his third marriage to a woman who had become too dour and sharp-tongued for his tastes.

They were introduced to one another briefly at a cocktail party at Tanya's sprawling villa by the sea. It was Tanya's gregarious husband, Agung, who had called out to her: 'Mama, come say hello to this guy from your hometown.' She acquiesced with grace but she was never one to be overly affable with a newcomer. Especially if the newcomer happened to be a middle-aged man with a possessive young paramour. But it was customary for residents to show polite interest in the *tamu* no matter how flitting and casual the encounter. She held out her hand limply, uttered pleasantries and asked where they were staying and what sort of tourist destinations they were going to go, feigning interest in the answers: answers that she had already heard hundreds of times in various permutations over the past two decades.

She couldn't even remember what he said after they were introduced. She was still disconcerted by his firm handshake. A grasp too prolonged for her comfort. And he looked hard into her eyes as if he recognized her, like someone trying to retrieve a distant, significant memory.

She was out on the patio alone, looking for her golden retriever that was hiding somewhere in the garden. She walked all the way to the closest point to the beach, and then she stood enjoying the sea breeze in the darkness. She wondered if they had ever crossed paths in their old hometown, decades ago and thousands of miles away from this prime Bali beachfront property.

'So Tanya, do you ever miss home?' he asked, his voice startled her but she was quickly back into her hostess mode.

'No, not really. My family is here. My life is in Bali.'

Ken didn't say a word, he only looked at her, his head cocked to one side, a small smile playing on his rather full lips. It made her shiver ever so slightly and she shrugged the sensation off almost defiantly. He made her feel self-conscious about her copper-coloured lace *kebaya* and the silk hand-painted batik sarong. He was smiling now as if he saw her as she used to be, as a gauche teenager, with her blonde braids and braces. No one had ever made her feel so exposed before. No one had ever made her feel like an impostor.

Ever so quietly, as if whispered, he said in Indonesian, '*Hidupmu adalah dengan ku.*'

A female voice resounded from the inner courtyard of the villa, the voice becoming louder as his lover came closer to where they were. 'Ken, are you out there? Darling, my poor legs can't take any more of this. It's brutal how these mosquitoes are singling me out. Please take me back to the hotel.'

When they had left she mulled over the words Ken had whispered in Indonesian. It was overly flirtatious, and so overtly inappropriate. Something that would normally have made her cringe or burst out loud in laughter, incredulous. 'Your life is with me.' Who says things like that anyway? Your life is with me? And to say the words in Indonesian – was he mocking her life as the wife of an Indonesian man?

She almost told her husband Agung what Ken had said. Agung was an easy-going man, more likely to take it with good humour than to explode in a fit of jealousy but she didn't feel like

sharing those words with him. In a perverse way it would feel like a betrayal had she informed Agung. A betrayal to Ken: a man she barely knew. A man she hardly even trusted, but nevertheless a man from a place she once called home.

* * *

Her husband owned a successful furniture manufacturing business, producing teak wood furniture and mock-antique pieces for Europe and North America. He was now toying with the idea of going into politics but she wasn't too keen on the regular absences in Jakarta that such a position would entail. When Tanya met Agung, twenty-five years ago, she was on holiday right after her college graduation. She was a girl of twenty-one with plans of becoming a counsellor at a high school in a town nearby when she returned from her six-month holiday around the world. She remembered how her family were bitterly opposed to her travel plans because they were afraid for her, but she had saved for it since she was thirteen and then there were the graduation gifts of money from her proud grandmother and plane tickets from her favourite uncle for graduating magna cum laude.

She was a gangly middle child who was more likely to be in the library then out partying. She had had only one boyfriend in college and they split up when she was at the end of her sophomore year. She couldn't really remember who called it off but she clearly remembered him saying once, in quite a matter-of-fact way, that it was a good thing she had brains because she was average-looking. The words stung her even though she had laughed when he had said them. After the break-up she found

herself with more time for studying but she also made an effort to better herself with tapes and books on self-improvement as well as a series of makeovers in various department stores in the big city. She promised herself that her life was going to be anything but average.

Agung was twenty-eight, working for his father at their small shop selling furniture supplied by several craftsmen from villages nearby. He had an easy way about him; he had the endearing quality of someone so comfortable in his own skin. He worked long hours at the shop but somehow he arranged it so that he could always find some time to spend with Tanya. He drove her all around the island to small villages tucked away on mountainsides and took her swimming at hidden beaches where the black sand glittered like crushed gemstones under the sun. He brought her to little-known temples where villagers, dressed in their very best traditional clothes, were gathered for prayers. He was attentive and always a gentleman and he spoke his English carefully and courteously. He was ambitious with big plans to grow his father's business by marketing to more foreign customers. He was unlike any other boy she had known back home. He was self-possessed, proud of his heritage, of his island and yet he was humble and kind.

Bali was totally different to the life Tanya knew. She was used to a simple structured existence where everything and everyone functioned as they were supposed to. Back home people spoke plainly and honestly; ostentation and drama were not normal, everything was solid and functional. In Bali, every nook, every corner harboured something ornate and surprising, like the intricate roof decorations, the meticulously carved doorways, the

gilded home temples and the chequered or yellow cloths lovingly placed around statues. She was delighted each time she saw the men from the village, all of them in theatrical make-up, a big hibiscus behind an ear and in their bright shiny costumes, riding off on their motorbikes to their nightly dance performance for the tourists. There were no bashful smiles, no explanations. It was all so matter of fact and routine.

She was drawn to the way their beautiful stone sculptures were placed in every home, at every sacred space, not merely in museums or the town square as it was back home. And there were so many beliefs and superstitions and daily rituals that intrigued her. She was amazed at how the little baskets of offerings were made each day by the women. She appreciated how they had divided the day by three prayer times of the *Puja Trisandya*: at six in the morning as the sun rose, at noon, and again at six in the evening as the night gently settled on the island. She envied the beautiful, graceful figures of the women clad in their revealing lace *kebayas* over black corsets and their tight-fitting sarongs, carrying their multi-tiered multi-coloured offerings on their heads, straight-backed and nonchalant.

When she realised Agung was falling in love with her, she was overcome with relief. She knew Bali and her people had beguiled her with such intensity that she just couldn't imagine ever having to leave it. She had to endure several long, tearful telephone conversations with her parents to explain why she wanted to postpone her trip home and each time she felt even more impatient and alien to everything her home stood for. And so when Agung proposed to her only forty-five days after they met, she said a resolute yes. They were married exactly five months after they

met on a day that was deemed auspicious by the priest and his ancient palm-leaf calendar. Her family tried to dissuade her but to no avail. She never wanted to look back.

Here she stood almost head and shoulders above the other women. Her blonde hair was like spun gold in the sunlight, a perfect foil for the beautiful *kebaya*s and sarongs that she wore every day. She made it her mission to learn the high-caste Balinese dialect that Agung's family spoke. She made an effort to learn how to make the daily offerings from the women although her creations were never as delicate as they should have been. It really pleased her in-laws and her husband that she was so keen to learn all that was necessary to become a bona fide Balinese wife.

They had two children in quick succession after they were married. It was soon apparent that living in the compound, where three generations of the family lived, was getting to be too much for her despite her best intentions of fully adopting the local way of life. She soon discovered that she still needed plenty of privacy and personal space in her own home. She was so grateful that Agung had understood that the best move was for them to build their own house to accommodate their own growing family. And so they moved down to the coast to his mother's ancestral land because they were both quite fond of the sea. There was quite a commute each time there was a religious ceremony at their village or family temple but fortunately Agung's business was located about half way between his family compound and their sprawling beach property.

Now twenty-six years later, she hadn't quite become the Balinese woman she had wanted to be as an idealistic twenty-two-year-old girl but she had made her peace with the culture

and the people she had adopted. For the first few years, she had joined all the religious ceremonies and rituals faithfully but as the children were growing up, the demands on her time had also increased. There was all the ferrying she had to do to bring them to their expensive international school, and then back, and some days there were the extra-curricular activities: violin or soccer or taekwondo. And also on weekends: the requisite Balinese language and dance classes that she and Agung had insisted on for fear their children would grow up too westernised. She had also found a group of expatriate women and foreign wives like her whom she called her closest friends and so she slowly drifted away from her husband's family even though relations were still quite cordial.

Her beautiful children, Surya and Arjuna, were now living abroad, a choice they made after they had graduated and found their big-city jobs. They had made their way to her own family and they were now very close to her aging parents. The kids would come back to Bali for their annual holidays but they had made it very clear that they preferred their lifestyle and all the amenities of the West, and most of all, they enjoyed their freedom away from the cultural strictures of a traditional Balinese life and the smallness of island living.

She understood how they felt but all the same their absence from the huge villa and the comfortable life Agung and she had built for them made her feel hurt and abandoned. Her Balinese in-laws would probably tell her it was karma for the hurt she had caused her parents by leaving home years ago. She tried talking to Agung about how she was feeling – usually with tears welling in her eyes – but he would just hug her and quickly change the

subject to something more mundane like the lawn or their dogs or the family SUV needed servicing. He missed them too but he had his friends, men he had known since their childhood days in the village.

* * *

She didn't see Ken again for almost two years after their first meeting. Then one day, as she had just finished her solo yoga session out on her patio facing the beachfront, the phone in the living room rang.

'Ibu Tanya? Do you remember me?' She recognised his voice in an instant but she didn't want to give him the pleasure of thinking that he was that memorable.

'No, I'm sorry. May I know to whom I'm speaking?' she said in the most aloof tone that she could muster.

'Aaaah, yes ... I understand ... well, it's Ken, Dr Ken Thatcher, we met briefly a couple of years ago at a party at your house?' he said, wearily, almost as if he knew this was a pantomime that he had to play along with. 'Do you remember me?'

She kept silent for a moment, not knowing why his voice made her feel breathless.

'Ken from back home? Oh yes ... how are you? And how is Elizabeth?'

'I'm fine. I expect Elizabeth is fine wherever she may be now. I haven't seen her in over a year actually.'

'How can I help you, Ken?' And as soon as she had uttered those words, she regretted it. She didn't want to sound like an overly obliging housewife with nothing better to do.

'As a matter of fact there is something you can help me with. I need your expertise, your advice ... on a piece of land I'm thinking of buying. Not far from where you live actually.'

She tried to think of all the reasons why she wouldn't be able to help him but she couldn't think of any.

'I'll help you, we'll see this piece of land together and I'll tell you what I think,' she said trying her best to conceal the quiver in her voice. And with those words, their liaison took life.

* * *

He said that from the moment they first met, he knew that they would one day become lovers. He promised her that he would always be there for her no matter what she decided. He told her that he intended to live the rest of his days in Bali, relishing whatever time they could steal to be with each other. She was acutely aware that she was the wife of a Balinese businessman who was quite well known in her town; and that her husband had friends and family with a reach that was island-wide. Even now she couldn't be sure that someone in this sleepy fishing village on the northeast Bali coast wasn't relaying information to her husband that she was sharing a room – the most secluded one in this small beach resort – with another man. This big *bule* man who had made her moan and howl in pleasure; this man who had her imploring him not to stop.

He had undressed her as soon as they were over the threshold. He slammed the door shut and pushed her towards the bed as he impatiently unzipped her dress and tossed it to a corner of the room. An hour later, after their desire was spent, she was lying,

or rather half sitting, astride him on the big sofa, and she glanced at the untidy heap of dress, bra, boxers, pants, shirt, panties, all jumbled up together; it made her smile.

'What are you smiling at, you shameless harlot?'

'Your messiness, old man. No silly young intern to pick up after you in this hotel room,' she pointed to the pile as she extricated herself from his inert body, moving her leg that seemed to be entwined with his arm.

'No, not yet, let me stay in you …' She ignored him, clambered off the sofa and tiptoed to the bathroom with her back to him; she was now acutely conscious of every piece of flab and cellulite marring his view of her body.

After she had showered, she found him on the veranda facing the beach, his boxers were back on him and he was chugging a bottle of water. He belched in her direction for effect and grinned.

'I feel like a new man. Let's go take a dip in the sea. Skinny-dip?' he said as he walked to her and pulled the towel off her body in one firm tug as if he was a magician performing for a crowd.

She demurred, insisting that she was freshly showered but he ignored her protestations: he just swept her off her feet as if she was weightless, and tossed her on the bed.

'You're a crazy old man, you'll put your back out. Let me get some clothes on.'

'No, no … you won't need any clothes on this trip. And I am crazy. I'm crazy for you, my brazen harlot. We'll make sweet love all weekend long until you can't walk …' he laughed. And she laughed too at his absurd recklessness.

'You know you won't be able to do anything so soon. So

enough with the big talk, old man.'

He dove beside her to reach the bedside table and proudly showed her the Viagra tablets.

'No rest for the wicked, Ibu.'

She giggled as he climbed on top of her and showered kisses on her face, her chest and stomach.

Their peals of laughter broke through the night where only the sounds of the surf and the cackle of a lone gecko could be heard.

Hours later, they were still in bed, post-coitus, sweaty and naked and thirsty. She was half asleep under the covers, and he was stroking her head gently as if she were a baby.

'What are we doing? What does this all mean?' she asked drowsily.

'I don't know. We have a great time together. We talk. We laugh. A lot. We make love. Does it have to mean something?' He was about to say more when the first tremors began. He stopped and looked at her.

'It's nothing, probably a quake in Sulawesi or Flores somewhere,' she reassured him but then the shaking became stronger. The glass on the window panes juddered violently as if withstanding strong gusts of wind. The sturdy teak bed they were on started rocking back and forth, creaking ominously.

'We should get out of here, get away from the coast. What if there's a tsunami?' he said as he picked up their clothes and stuffed everything into his duffel bag. 'Come, quick, get your things, let's go. Now!'

She could only nod; she was overcome with fear. But more than anything it was the fear of having her dead body discovered

here by her husband; naked but for a thin bed sheet, with this man by her side. What would the kids think? What would Agung's family say?

* * *

She arrived home past midnight, after she had dropped Ken off at his rented villa. All the lights in the study were on. She took off her shoes on the veranda and walked into the house quietly. Agung was sitting at his desk poring over some handwritten ledgers and looking at a spreadsheet on the computer screen. He looked weary and old. She just stood at the door watching him until he realised she was there.

'Where have you been, Mama?' he asked, taking off his glasses to rub his eyes.

'I thought I told you I would be looking at some property around the island?'

'Where? In Karangasem or Lovina? Who were you with? Dr Ken?'

She was about to lie but she thought the better of it. She just nodded.

'I thought you said you'd be in Jakarta till Tuesday. Have you had dinner? Do you want me to make you something?'

'My meeting with Bapak Supriyadi was cancelled last minute: there's a crisis in West Java he had to attend to – so I cut my trip short.

'Shall I fix you something quick to eat?'

'No, I've eaten – I had some *bebek betutu* in Sanur, with Gede.'

'In that case, I'll just shower and go straight to bed. I'll probably sleep in the downstairs room – I've got a very early yoga session tomorrow morning.'

'I'll be turning in soon too. I'm too tired to make sense of these numbers.'

She was about to walk out of the study but she turned back to remind him about insurance payments that were due soon. He was now half slumped over his desk, rubbing his temple distractedly. She walked back to his side and gave him a long kiss on the top of his head.

He grimaced, 'I can smell him on you, Ma.' He said shaking his head. 'That man smokes too much.'

'Yes, he does.'

'It's not good for you,' he said, still shaking his head.

* * *

Tanya was up before the alarm on her mobile phone pealed with the simulated sounds of birds chirping at dawn. She lay on her back looking at the ceiling, thinking of Ken and what it would be like to wake up with him each and every day of her life. She liked the way he slept naked, after tossing off his boxer shorts or pyjama pants just before he pulled up the sheets to his chest. She liked the way his hand reached out for her body even when he was deep in slumber. She liked the way he could arouse her with his big, warm hands even when he was half asleep.

She let out a big sigh as she jumped out of the bed, shaking off her thoughts of Ken and their love-making. She knew she was behaving like a hormonal teenager instead of a middle-aged

woman with a husband and two grown children.

After a quick shower, she walked through the first floor of the house, still dark and silent in the early hours, to retrieve her yoga mat by the front door. She stepped on something that pierced her foot and the sharp pain made her cry out. Her foot was bleeding. She saw that the cut was from a sapphire blue glass shard – she recognised it as part of a crystal bowl her grandmother had given her for her wedding decades ago. It was a beloved heirloom that she had wanted to pass on to her daughter. Did her housekeeper break it? Or was it the earthquake?

'I Luh? Are you awake? I Luh, can you please come here for a moment, please?' she shouted in the direction of the kitchen and the housekeeper's bedroom.

It was a few minutes before I Luh appeared, hair dishevelled, a towel draped over her bare shoulders and a faded sarong secured above her ample breasts.

'What happened, what's the problem?' I Luh rushed to her, rubbing the sleep from her eyes.

'Did you break this, my blue bowl from my grandmother?'

'Ohhh, that! No, it wasn't me. You'll have to ask your husband – he was the last one holding it.'

'When?'

'Yesterday, right after the earthquake. You know how scared I get during a quake. I screamed for everyone to get out and I ran to the road in front of the house.'

'Yes, I know how you act every time there's an earthquake,' Tanya glared at I Luh.

'Well, after that, I came in here to check on the things in the living room in case anything was broken, and he was in here, he

was holding pieces of the bowl. Nothing else was broken in here. I checked, Ibu Jero.'

He was holding pieces of the bowl. Nothing else was broken in here. Those words reverberated in her head. All sound was drowned out by the weight of those words. Did her husband deliberately break the bowl? Why would he? Anger? Spite? It was so out of character for her genial, even-tempered husband. And to confront him would be out of question. There would be no way back if harsh words and accusations were exchanged between them.

* * *

He knows.

It was difficult for her to maintain her yoga *asana*s with her bandaged foot throbbing and her emotions in turmoil. Could it be possible that Agung knew of the affair? She had tried to be as careful as possible about her assignations with Ken out of respect for her husband. And frankly, out of plain selfishness, because she did not want to lose the comfortable life that she and Agung had made over their two decades together. She didn't want to lose her beautiful sprawling house, the shiny SUVs at her disposal, all her gold and diamond jewellery or her stature in this part of the island. She was the esteemed Ibu Jero to everyone and it counted for something.

He knows.

What if Agung knew? Would he destroy everything they had built together just to assuage his wounded male pride. Agung was pragmatic and he was never one to let passions or impulsive

behaviour guide his actions or his speech. All these years his speech, his actions, have been guided by temperance, by gentleness and by logic. This was the Agung she had known for all their life together. But there was that bowl, their precious wedding gift, now broken into smithereens. Agung knew how much she loved her grandmother; and just how much the crystal bowl meant to her. He couldn't have broken the bowl deliberately. Just the thought of her husband in an enraged state – enraged enough to smash her precious heirloom – made her shiver in the heat of day.

* * *

She found herself in front of Ken's house that afternoon; she waited in her car looking at his house from a safe distance. No one was about. The farmers were already home for the day. The sun was setting in the far corner of the rice fields. It would soon be harvest time for the farmers of this village. The fields were burnished with a deep golden glow and then transformed into a bright copper blaze as the sun sank closer to the horizon. From a distance a village priest intoned the *Puja Trisandya* for the evening. Even after decades of living in Bali such a view set against the sound of the mantra echoing through the ether made her catch her breath.

Ken was on one of his many sabbaticals, and this time to write a scholarly book about Bali's history with Chinese traders and how this had influenced Balinese culture through the generations. He had spent six months in Beijing researching as best he could, given his limited grasp of Mandarin. But he was now based in Bali indefinitely or until his money ran out, he had said in a cavalier tone. She was beginning to discern something more whenever that

tone appeared in their conversations: was it actually fear, or could it have been a tinge of defeat? She would always mentally shrug it off and chalk it up to her own anxieties and guilt. Ken was a survivor, after all.

She came out of the car as soon as the sun had disappeared beneath the horizon; by now the shadows had lengthened and darkness began to fill all the surrounding spaces. She walked to his front door and opened it quietly. Ken could never remember to lock the door even though she had reminded him over and over again. They had had this conversation again and again and each time he chalked up her fears to that of an overwrought rich white woman living in a Third World country, despite all her years here.

'Look, Bali isn't what it used to be, there've been quite a few cases. Someone could just walk in with a knife and rob you. Worse still you get hurt or killed. For what, a stupid laptop, an iPhone, a watch? Please be careful, please lock your doors,' she had entreated a few weeks ago. He had laughed her off with a big hug, scooping her onto his bed as if she was weightless. As always all her rational thought was subsumed by his passionate kisses and his expert ways of teasing her into easy submission. She had felt as if she was seventeen again, unsteady and gauche; governed solely by her biological imperative to give in to him.

* * *

She found him sitting in a big bamboo armchair, staring out of his veranda trying to blow smoke rings from his cigarillo. There was a lit green mosquito coil forced around the neck of a large beer bottle by his feet.

'I thought you'd be working,' she said, as she kissed him on the neck. He smelled of sweat, beer and cigarettes.

'I am working as a matter of a fact. I'm mulling over a new chapter. And how do you do? To what do I owe the pleasure of your unexpected company this evening?'

'You're working, without your laptop?' He squirmed in his chair at her question, a sure sign of his rising displeasure.

'Yes, I am working without my laptop.'

'Where is your laptop anyway?'

'So you've come all the way here, risking the suspicion and ire of your dearest husband, our Balinese Nobleman, merely to check on the whereabouts of my laptop? Was that the reason for this all important visit of the honourable Ibu Jero to my humble abode?'

She knew that she was now treading on perilous ground, she knew this each time he began to use that supercilious professorial tone with her. It was usually a precursor to one of his long sullen silences and she knew the only way to stave it off was to beat a hasty retreat.

'I was just asking. No need to get so annoyed with me.'

'Well, you've asked, so just leave it at that. You didn't happen to bring me any dinner with you? There's hardly any food in the pantry or in the fridge.'

'No, no I didn't, I'm sorry. I wasn't planning on being here too long. I have something disturbing to tell you. I think Agung knows about us.'

Ken didn't say a word. Nor did he look at her; he just continued smoking the cigarillo until it was about an inch long before flicking it out forcefully into the garden, still lit, the red ember marked a glowing arc into the bushes. He remained silent

and he lit another cigarillo with deliberation.

She told him the story about her smashed wedding crystal heirloom and how angry Agung must have been to do something like that. And that it would have been totally out of character for her gentle husband to be so enraged.

'So what are you saying? That I should fear for my life? What do you think he's likely to do? Do you think he's capable of killing an American citizen out of his newly found passions? Or is he the type to hire thugs from a nearby island to slit my throat?'

'I don't know. I honestly don't know. I've never been in this situation before. It's not like him at all but what if he kicks me out of my home? I only have that one bank account, the rest is in our joint account. I have all my jewellery. Really, I never ever wanted to hurt him. He's been a very decent man to me.'

'So what I'm hearing is that it all boils down to your worldly possessions over here? Is that so? Well, my dear, if you are left out on the street without so much as one *are* of land to your name, what will you do? There must be some kind of legal recourse for you. There must be other foreign wives in your predicament.'

'No, no, I don't really know of anyone else. At least I don't know them well. We don't exactly all sit down together to discuss and prepare for these worst-case scenarios. Most wives are looked after by their Balinese husbands and if they can't hack sharing their husbands with another woman then they leave. I don't know. I don't think leaving Bali is an option for me now. This is my home.'

'So if indeed your husband is aware that we're fucking each other, then what? I suppose there's no question of you moving in with me, to live with me in this villa?'

'Do you have to put it so crudely?'

'Well, what else do you think we're doing with each other? What else do you want to call this – how would you caption it? A grand middle-aged romance between a dissipated academic and a former small-town debutante? Don't be fooled by what this is just because we get to screw each other against this magical, tropical backdrop. It's just as sordid as it would be if we were doing it doggy-style in some sleazy motel off Highway 59 back home.'

'Stop it. Why do you have to make it sound so obscene?'

'Because it is. Any way you look at it, it is. Simply because you're willing to risk everything to have sex with me from time to time. Because you're still deluding yourself into thinking that you can't lose everything, you won't lose anything. You're just being greedy.'

'I'm greedy? I have more to lose than you do. You coast along in life, landing where you will, so perhaps you won't understand what's at risk. I've got roots here. I have a husband who loves me.'

'You have property here. You have a husband you're fond of. And now you also have me.'

'I have you?' She looked hard at him, trying to find the truth in his words. He averted his face from her gaze.

'Yes. For as long as this feels good for both of us.' He shrugged as he uttered these words. But there is something in his tone that made her catch her breath and she remained silent. He added softly, 'God, this island is small. Maybe I didn't realise just how small it is.'

'It's small if you have a secret …' she murmured, more to herself than to him.

They sat together in silence until all colour had left the sky

and it was a deep, dark indigo. The stars were sprinkled across it and the moon was just a sliver of light.

'My laptop got stolen.'

'Gosh! Was it stolen right here? Did you lose all your research? How about your paper?'

'I have backup files saved here and there. I suppose it won't be too difficult to piece together what I've written so far. It will take some time but it won't be impossible. Although there were photos that I can't replace.'

'What photos?'

'From my travels in China. People I interviewed for my book. Photos from Bali also for the book – the villages up north around Buleleng and in Singaraja town. Photos of us on our clandestine trips, photos of you, taken right here,' he shrugged, nonplussed.

'My photos? Clothed or unclothed? I thought I told you to delete those!'

'Relax. It was a few naked pictures. Your body is still as beautiful as a thirty-year-old. Nothing to feel embarrassed about.'

'It's got nothing to do with my vanity. What if those photos got into Agung's hands?'

'It won't. You live miles and miles away from here. No one knows you here.'

'You don't know that. The Balinese have a knack of knowing things.'

'What do you mean by knowing things? Through the village gossip mill? Or mystical knowing? Do you think the local shaman, our village *balian* here, is going to inform your husband? You're obviously over-reacting.'

'What do you think Agung would do if he saw those photos?

Did you even think of that? He would have every reason to kill us both!'

'Now you're being silly and melodramatic. Your Agung is not that kind of man – he's placid not passionate. I really don't have time to listen to these ridiculous housewife rantings. I have work to do.'

'Without your laptop?'

'Yes, without my laptop.' Saying these words seemed to make him even angrier. 'Now if you don't mind, I would like to get some work done. I have all these notes to transcribe.' With a few long strides he was at the front door, opening it wide for her to exit.

She fumbled for her handbag and struggled with the straps of her sandals and with hot tears spilling onto her cheeks, she rushed out without a backward glance.

* * *

Ken called her several times later that night but she put her phone on silent and let it ring on. That night she slept in the bedroom that she shared with Agung. Agung had called to say that he was with his friends in Seminyak to have dinner at a Japanese restaurant and to watch his favourite jazz band performing. She remembered the days when it was their weekly routine as a couple to enjoy live music performances all around the island, from Nusa Dua to Ubud and down to Sanur, Kuta and Seminyak. During those halcyon days, they were a well-known pair in those nightspots; each outing eased by fine wines and the best food served on the island. They never seemed to run out of stories to tell each other

and their love for each other enveloped them like a force field.

This changed when the children left Bali for college in the US. Each phone call, each email and each summer vacation marked a growing distance between them and their children. And then there was nothing they could do but to lose their beautiful Surya and Arjuna to the bright, wide spaces and opportunities that the US offered. Their son and daughter were never coming back to stay except for their frenzied Bali holidays every couple of years, and always accompanied by their American friends and cousins. And each time Surya and Arjuna left, their sprawling ocean-side villa always seemed even bigger and emptier than before.

*　*　*

She lay in bed and she tried to will herself to sleep but sleep continued to elude her. She tried to slow her breathing and she tried to synchronise her breath to the sound of the waves audible through her open windows but she could only hear Ken's dismissive tone and how it made everything feel so wrong.

At about 3 am, Agung came back. He tried hard to be quiet but he kept knocking into the furniture – she could hear his muffled swearing as he stubbed his toe into the chair and bumped his knee into the dresser. As always he was conscientious about keeping the lights off and his noise levels down so as not to wake her up. She heard him in the bathroom, singing softly to himself, it was an old Indonesian *keroncong* ballad. He stumbled back into the bedroom and right into bed. She pretended to be asleep, hugging a pillow to her side of the bed. He rolled right next to her and he kissed her on the back of her head. 'I still love you, Ma, even

though you don't love me anymore.' Within a few seconds, he was back on his side of the bed, and then his snoring reverberated in the bare spaces of the huge bedroom suite.

* * *

Agung was still asleep when she left the house. She hurriedly dressed and rushed out to Ken's villa after listening to his voice messages on her phone. There were too many and so she only chose to hear the most recent ones.

'Tanya, I need to speak to you.' 'Look, I know I was a complete jerk yesterday. There's no excuse for my behaviour.' 'Why aren't you returning my calls? I've left you countless messages.' 'Where the hell are you, Tanya?' 'Are you all right? Did Agung say anything to you?' Tanya, will you please come over to see me as soon as you get this message?' 'I need to see you immediately, please come over to my villa.' 'Please, please call me. It's urgent.' Ken's tone was increasingly frantic as the messages piled on. In his most recent messages, he sounded breathless with anxiety.

When she arrived at the villa, the front doors were thrown wide open and there was a Balinese woman sweeping in front of the threshold. Ken's rented Suzuki Jimny was not in the garage. The woman dropped her broom and came out to see Tanya as she walked through the driveway.

'Are you Ibu Tanya? Bapak Ken has left Bali. He said he won't be back. He's taken all his things with him.'

'Where did he go? Do you know when he left?'

'He didn't say where. He was in a big rush. His friends, two Balinese men, came to pick him up very early this morning.'

'Friends? Do you know their names? And what's happened to his Jimny?'

'I'm sorry, I don't know, they're not from around here and they didn't introduce themselves. Someone picked up the Jimny after they all left.'

She couldn't even respond to what the woman said. Tanya just nodded her head and left the compound, driving as fast and as far away as she could.

For hours she drove around aimlessly; driving through Ubud, then Klungkung and right up to small mountain roads near Sidemen and she circled back, until she found herself at home. She had thought about going to the airport but if he had left at dawn, his flight would have long departed.

Agung was not in when she arrived and she was glad for that. She checked her voicemail repeatedly but there was nothing new from Ken. She listened to his messages again and again, trying to find some clues from his words, from the cadences of his voice. He was definitely agitated. Perhaps, there was even restrained anger. She could also detect a hint of real regret in his words. Beyond that there was absolutely no intimation as to where he was headed and why he had left so suddenly. He had just vanished without as much as a brief note explaining why to her.

That night she dreamt that Ken had phoned her and she took his call at an old payphone in a hazy place that looked like a small school in a mountainside village near Sidemen, but the children who milled around her were American – blondes, brunettes, redheads – all Caucasian kids who looked like the ones she might have played with when she was in elementary school. The connection was very bad and it kept cutting off and then back

on; the kids were noisy and she could scarcely make out what he was saying but she thought she heard him say that he was home. He had to go home to settle some business but she couldn't hear what business.

The dream ended abruptly after he said, 'I love you, Tanya.' It was as if her subconscious knew how implausible it was for him to utter those words. She woke up startled and in tears. She looked across to see Agung on his side, sound asleep, his back was facing her, his body almost on the edge of their king-sized bed.

* * *

For days that ran into weeks, she scoured the local newspapers: she wondered if there was any news of bodies found in the rice fields or washed ashore; bodies of Caucasian men of Ken's age. There was nothing in any of the papers and it gave her succour. There was a suicide case in a small Kuta hotel but the man was a sixty-seven-year-old German.

Ken had most probably returned to the US. But she had no way of knowing where he could be. He was, after all, an itinerant scholar, with work based in several states, with estranged wives and adult children across a number of continents. She didn't even know where to start looking for him. He was a man who took pride in living in the present; he was very reticent about divulging his past life and his past relationships. Every so often, when he was drunk or tired, he would let slip tantalising morsels of information and then he would change the subject quickly when he realised that he had revealed too much. She knew the name of the last university he was attached to in the US but that was it. She

thought of flying home to look for him starting at that university but it could well be a wasted journey if no one knew anything and worse still, if he found out she was tracking him and he got very angry with her for invading her privacy.

As the weeks wore on, Tanya became even more certain that a trip to the US would give her the peace of mind she desperately sought. She needed to know why Ken had left and where he had ended up after Bali. He once told her that he disliked drama and that all his relationships dissolved into nothingness rather than end in an explosion of passion or rancour. But despite what he claimed, Tanya knew there was acrimony; from what little she could piece together, his wives and former lovers did not want to have anything to do with him. There was no vestige of affection between them – even amongst his children. They had divested Ken from their lives and they had carried on, some of them let go so hurriedly and so resolutely, they didn't even demand from him their alimony or child support payments. It was almost as if they had wanted to excise him completely out of their lives like a malignant tumour.

In a perverse way, Ken's solitary state, his rootless journeying around the world made her heart ache for him even more. All she knew about life was centred on growing roots: creating a family, making a beautiful home and being a member of a larger community, and then came along a man who was such a dismal failure at making these human connections work. A man so self-regarding that he wasn't even aware of all he had lost along the way. She felt deeply for his failures even though he seemed to be unscathed by it all.

She mulled over her options as she tried to find the courage

to tell Agung that she wanted to make a trip back to the US. She would use her children and her aged parents to justify the trip; surely these would be good enough reasons for her husband to allow her to be away for a month. She thought a month would be enough time for her to track Ken, and perhaps if his trail was too difficult for her to trace, she would even hire a private investigator.

For all this she would need money. She had a personal account at one of the local banks and while there wasn't enough money in there for her to start a new life, there certainly was more than enough funds for her travel plans and a few months' worth of living expenses for anywhere in the world. And there was her jewellery.

Tanya planned to call her travel agent, withdraw as much money as she could from her bank account and then she would tell Agung about her trip. She was about to call the agent when she discovered that she didn't have her number in her mobile phone directory. She was quite sure that Agung had kept the travel agent's business card in a folder in his home office.

She went into his office to look for the card but she was taken aback. All his files were haphazardly strewn around the big teak table; this was very unusual for her husband who had always been meticulous about his files and the tidiness of his office. Her knees felt weak and she sat in his chair for a while. The condition of his desk filled her with a deep sense of disquiet. It was almost as if it displayed a gaping fault line in all that was now amiss in their world.

Her hands were shaking as she continued looking for the travel agent's card. She couldn't find the plastic folder that contained all the business cards. It was usually placed on the top

right side of the desk, always positioned parallel to the phone-fax machine with almost military precision. The machine was now buried under a stack of papers and unopened letters. There was a folder right on top of the pile marked 'Withdrawal' and it fell right off the desk onto the floor. When she bent down to pick up the contents, there was one bank withdrawal slip that stood out because it was relatively new; the paper was still crisp and the computer printout still clear in contrast to the other slips.

The amount was for 100,000 US dollars, withdrawn in cash for 'Dr K', dated the day before Ken vanished from her life. She was quite certain that she was meant to find that withdrawal slip. Almost as certain as she was then, that she would never find Ken.

MEMBER OF THE CLUB

BON VIVANT FOR HIRE

I have never thought of Bali as paradise on earth. Not once. Bali was just pleasant and different and it suited me. The decision to stay here for the rest of my life had nothing to do with wanting to act out some kind of lurid expat fantasy. Rather it came about because I had opted for a complete change in my lifestyle. I know that some of my friends from my old life (the life that started in Kuta, moved up to Seminyak and ended in Canggu) were worried that I had 'gone native'; although the term itself is so insultingly stupid that I just had to laugh it off. This new way of living offers me something I've never been able to get before. It was inevitable that I would choose the new life. I was careening along aimlessly, a world-class hedonist, or as my fat friend Dale once described me, 'A world-class donkey's arse.' From beach to beach, from club to club, from girl to girl, from upset to upset.

All the partying was of course interspersed with my wretched attempts at rehabilitation. Desperate acts of contrition, both emotional and physical. The colonic irrigation up in Ubud – I saw all my faeces being 'cleansed' out of my gut and all I wanted to do was run out of the place, screaming in sheer disgust. The three-day detox program in Canggu (which was swiftly followed by a three-day drinking and fornicating binge in Sanur, if I may

add). The week-long yoga retreat – which was mellow and replete with cute hippie girls but still not compelling enough to keep me entranced for the entire duration. Perhaps it was the 4.30 am meditation sessions. Or perhaps it was the rigour and boredom of exercise and concentration whilst I was actually more interested in the arresting contours of a girl's shapely bottom in the front row.

But as with many hedonists who are not fortunate enough to be born as heirs or heiresses, I found out that I had run out of money but the thought of having to go home to a bleak winter, tail between my legs, was too much to bear. I had made quite a few friends and it wasn't too hard to find a small project or two that needed a personable bloke who could be charming and responsible enough to get the job done. Real estate broker. Sourcing agent. Event organiser. Travel companion. Procurer at large. Like most of my relationships, none of these jobs was permanent. And then it hit me. I had become one of those infamous Bali-based hustlers, a bon vivant for hire. And the thought of becoming, one day, soon, an aging bon vivant for hire was too scary for me to contemplate. I could just imagine the older, much worse-for-wear me – greyer, more wrinkled than a Shar-Pei – trudging along on my arthritic knees; the old prostate showing its first signs of frailty, making me have to piss every chance I could get; whilst all the time having to cadge business from unwilling tourists and suspicious newcomers. Too, too sad …

I think my bourgeois upbringing kicked in right about then. I knew then I needed more stability. My dad who has run and owned a pub for most of his adult life would have been proud. I needed regular income and a retirement plan that precluded

living like an indigent on the beach. I started my own business: I became a bona fide sourcing agent for furniture and housewares. Yes, there were many other expats doing the same thing in Bali but the pie was sufficiently big that there was still room for a new, resourceful and hard-working player to make good money. It took almost a year and a half for me to begin seeing some real profits. I hired a couple of my Balinese friends, Made and Ngurah, to help me out with the operations. I trusted these two men more than I did my own family. I dare say they close to worshipped me for taking them away from their dead-end jobs and giving them the opportunity to earn more money than they could ever imagine. We were all set for a brand new shiny life as only Bali could help create.

Love and the fortune-teller

The first year and a half was mostly hard work but we laid the groundwork for the business to grow. Things were going well when I met and fell in love with a girl. A beautiful Indonesian girl whose father was from Sulawesi and mother from Bali. I was completely blind-sided. I dare say my focus for the job was less than optimum during the heady days of the romance. To think that it all started off as a bit of a laugh. She definitely knew how to keep me coming back for more. I don't quite know what it was. Perhaps it was because she had an air of nonchalance that kept me hooked. And she wasn't exactly chatty but she was definitely funny. A pretty girl who could make me chuckle. I don't know when her nonchalance became detachment. But it did. She seemed quieter when we were together. Sometimes even aloof. As if she had a lot on her mind. I was quite smitten with her by then. Made

and Ngurah were always a bit wary of her but they didn't say anything except for their usual, 'Have fun but *hati-hati';* which is their ever courteous and understated Balinese way of saying: 'Be careful, you bloody idiot!'

How could I have not seen it coming? I was so sure she wasn't a gold-digger. She was sexy in an understated, well-dressed and self-contained sort of way. And she had a good enough job managing a small boutique hotel in Jimbaran. She never asked me for any money for herself. There was never any tiresome conversation about a family member who needed emergency funds to start a business or to settle a debt or pay off a recruiter for a job on a cruise ship. Yes, you live here long enough and you would have heard them all. She wasn't mercenary. Or so I thought. The truth was there was a bigger fish to fry. And so she left me for an old geezer with assets in at least three different resort islands spread over two continents. She didn't even bother to tell me in person. My rude awakening came about from a caption to a photo of her and her new man in one of those Bali society pages. 'Mr So-and-so and his new fiancée, Ms So-and-so.' Fait accompli.

I chose not to confront her. After all, what good could come of that? Instead I went on a drinking binge at several bars and clubs on the Double Six stretch in Seminyak like I hadn't in a long time. Paralytic. And I spent at least two days recuperating at home, feeling more despondent than a teenage girl who just got cheated on by her boyfriend and her best friend. The business suffered a fair bit after my romantic debacle. I couldn't really focus and I guess I had some anger issues to work out. I kept losing my temper with Made and Ngurah. I lost my temper with our clients. I had trouble sleeping. And my gastritis felt as if it had

turned into a full-blown ulcer.

The turning point came one night after I had gone drinking at Ku De Ta. It's quite the tourist hangout but I thought I needed a change from my usual drinking-holes. Plus the place always had an assortment of beautiful girls from Jakarta who liked the chill-out ambience and that upscale beach scene. And there I was positioned strategically at the bar, scoping the action along the lounge chairs, hoping to catch the eye of one of the babes without a male escort. But they didn't even look at me. Well, maybe they did. Actually I'm almost sure one did: this beautiful girl with long straight hair, gave me the once-over and then she turned to her friends, whispered something which made all of them giggle. Did they think I looked pathetic, I wondered? Did they smell the desperation in the way I leaned against the bar? Or perhaps it was the way I gripped my glass of vodka?

So I failed to score that night. The only thing I succeeded in doing was to inflict further damage on my already battered ego. I was losing my ability to pull in the ladies. I stopped at the liquor shop on the way home and I stocked up on some more vodka. Stolichnaya. The poison of choice for my gulag of despair. I didn't even bother with dinner that evening. I just sat on my veranda, looking out on the symmetry of my two frangipani trees in full bloom and the perfect rectangle of my black marble plunge pool and my designer all-weather outdoor furniture and I just kept on drinking. I remember calling Made and Ngurah at some point in that long, lonely night and I could hear the concern in their voices.

'I think you drink enough, Scott. Better you go sleep now,' coaxed Made, and then Ngurah tried soothing me with: 'Don't make yourself sick just because of woman.'

I woke up close to noon with a mother of all hangovers. Still feeling sorry for myself, I dragged myself into work at about 1.30 pm and the boys were holding the fort quite well. I had trained them well. (Or maybe they had trained me, eh?) I wore my sunglasses indoors that day because the slightest exposure to light or noise just made my head throb as if there were ten *gamelan* bands playing with great gusto in my head. Everybody at the office kept a safe distance from me. I looked at the books, made sure all our numbers tallied and checked on all the email orders. Even after all these years I was meticulous about following up on the foreign orders. The Europeans were the worst if an order went amiss: the French would definitely take the trophy for being the most difficult customers and the last thing I wanted to deal with was how someone in my office or at the freight forwarders' screwed up some irate Frenchman's order.

I worked non-stop for about three hours and then I noticed Made hovering in the doorway. He was holding a huge cardboard file and he was looking at me with a strange expression: a combination of curiosity and pity.

'Did you want me to take a look at something, Made, or did you want to just stand there and keep staring at me?' I asked him, that familiar irritability had begun to worm itself back to my senses.

He shook his head, his radiant smile disarming me as it always did. 'No, no. I just wanted to make sure you're okay,' he replied gently. 'And ... I wanted to ask you to come with me to meet someone, a holy man. He read *lontar* leaves and he can give you some guidance.'

'Come on, Made, you know how I feel about all that mumbo-

jumbo magic stuff ... it may work for your people but I'm *bule*. It'll be a waste of time and money.'

'Just come with me, please, Scott. Spare one afternoon. It will change your life. Make you better,' he entreated, with that big unwavering smile.

I shrugged, having learnt from my Balinese friends that sometimes the best response is neither an outright 'yes' nor a 'no'.

THE CHANGELING

Did the holy man change my life? No, he didn't. But he seemed to have some special divination skills. Or maybe someone from my family or one of my ex-girlfriends was feeding him all the information. Far-fetched but who knows? My stubborn Western mind was still clutching onto some explanation that didn't have mystical or magical origins. But he told me a lot about my past and with accuracy that made me break out in cold sweat. But I refused to let my guard down. He told me that my path in life was actually very different from anything I had envisaged and that was why I was summoned to Bali. Summoned. Strange word but it was his, not mine. I nodded, trying very hard to look nonchalant. He kept smiling at me, an avuncular expression of concern. Understanding. And it made me inexplicably angry.

I just grabbed Made's hand as the holy man went on: 'You won't know peace until you spend some time at the ashram. You must go there. Don't wait.'

I put my hands together and in a bowing position I thanked him and backed myself out of the room. I mouthed a silent 'Let's get out of here' to Made but he ignored me. I left the holy man's compound, desperately in need of a smoke and a shot of whiskey.

Made took his time with the holy man. The old guy was probably giving him an earful about the recalcitrant *bule* he had brought. I hoped that Made didn't lose too much face by bringing me to meet the holy man. But he probably didn't. Knowing the Balinese as well as I have over the past six years, I know that I would be excused, as a foreigner, of a multitude of transgressions that would probably cause a local to be ostracised.

I don't really know what the holy man meant about 'peace' but from the time I visited him, I couldn't seem to get a decent night's sleep. I would toss and turn for the entire night, thinking of a thousand and one things in my life that had gone wrong: the girl I had lost, clients I had pissed off, my mum and dad and how I had disappointed them over the years, teachers in school who had called me a lost cause. Every damn screw-up in my miserable, misguided life.

My thoughts made me sit up in bed, distraught. I turned on the lights and smoked three cigarettes before I felt relaxed again. But what little sleep I got was troubled by a series of disconnected dreams. Little convoluted vignettes that started off plausibly enough but then would take distressing, improbable turns, involving people I knew whom were long dead or places that couldn't possibly exist. I was always late, or lost, having missed a flight, or a lift, or the bus, or a turning in the road. I got up from one such dream, sobbing like an abandoned child, and believe me when I say, I am definitely not the crying type.

I don't really know why I did it, but after that dream, I lit five sticks of incense. I waved it around the house like a feckless fool. I suppose I did it with the vain hope that it might dispel any last bit of disturbing energy still lurking about. I stuck the

incense in a big marble holder on the coffee table and watched them burn down to their wooden bits. I sat there in a semi-stupor watching the remaining smoke dissipate into the air, all scent of the sandalwood fast disappearing into the night. I heaved a long sigh of resignation because I knew what I had to do.

AFTER THE ASHRAM

The ashram changed me. But it wasn't like a bolt of lightning. There wasn't a grand epiphany that transformed me in an instant. It was more like a small candle that someone had lit in a dark, dark room and slowly you knew exactly where you were and what you were doing there. Gradual but much-needed clarity. I had gone without alcohol for a month and it didn't matter one bit. It was tough at first, acknowledging that I needed help. Me, Mr Self-Reliant, seeking clarity from a bunch of perpetually smiling, white-clad folks who looked as if they were floating along on a constant narcotic high. Who would have guessed?

They gave me a new name at the ashram. Sri Khrisna. At that point they could have given me a new nose and I wouldn't have cared one bit. I had relinquished all control. I had surrendered my free will for a greater good. It was liberating. I ate when they told me to eat, chanted mantras when they told me chant, cleaned when they told me to clean and slept when they told me to sleep. And did I ever sleep. The deep slumber of a newborn baby. But I gladly woke up at four every morning for meditation, without a single wise-crack, moan or a complaint. And so I floated along with the other ashram inmates – or as they preferred to call us, 'spiritual guests' – for one whole month.

The day before I left the ashram I had a long chat with one

of the gurus there, who was also my handler: Wayan Kerta, a skinny, smiley young man of about thirty. We spoke about so many things before I left but it wasn't as if he was imparting great truths for me to take to the outside world. It was a relaxed, desultory chat about meditation practice, diet and keeping sane without the supporting structure of the ashram. Towards the end of the session, he reached out and grabbed my hand. Of course I flinched, thinking, 'You've got the wrong number, mate ...' But he just gave me an even bigger smile as if he had guessed the reason for my discomfiture, and then he asked me, 'Tell me this, before you leave, why do you think you are in Bali?'

Why? What an odd question. To get as far away from home as possible. To escape the dreadful winters. To have a good time. To make some money. I shrugged because all the answers I could think of were feeble. He added pressure to his grip on my hand. 'Why?' he asked again. I shrugged again, clearly uncomfortable now. Silence. His smile was gone. He was now looking at me as if I was a science lab specimen. I felt tiny droplets of sweat trickle down my forehead, past the outer corner of my eyes. His grip on my hand tightened even more. 'You were meant to be here,' he said, relaxing his clasp before embracing me.

* * *

I took to wearing all-white after I left the ashram. Long sleeved cotton shirts, Indian cheese-cloth *kurta*s, tailored linen pants, loose drawstring cotton pants. Everything in white. In another life I would have taken the piss out of any Westerner with such affectations. But the white apparel was one tangible connection

to the thirty days I had spent in the ashram. In a strange way it anchored me. I added some plain wooden *mala* beads to my ensemble. One hundred and eight. I hold these between my fingers each time I feel my resolve faltering. Like that one night I ended up in a pub in Sanur.

I was at the bar and an ice-cold bottle of Storm beer stood facing me on the counter. And I took one swig. (It felt so good after my long dry spell.) Then I had two in quick succession. And another longer quaff, followed by a belch that shook my insides with a stunning vibrato. I dare say I must have cut quite a fine figure at the bar, resplendent in my most expensive white linen kit: long sleeved tunic top with satin trimmings and a pair of palazzo type pants made by a poncy Italian designer in Seminyak; a layer of *mala* beads with a silken red tassel that grazed the top of my navel; and a jaunty new *udeng*, the Balinese headgear worn by men for temple ceremonies and such.

A couple of the other pub regulars came to greet me; pats on the back, all hale and hearty, a couple of them even remarked on my apparel and of course, my absence from the drinking hole.

'What happened to you, mate? Feeling pure today, eh?' And: 'Well, well, look at you, all spiffed up, did you just come from a ceremony?' And: 'Nice threads, my friend. Where the hell have you been hiding? Haven't seen you around for yonks.' And: 'Jesus, look at this wanker in white! C'mon, you look as if you could do with a stiff drink ...'

I could only nod my head, trying my best to project an expression that was both enigmatic and beatific. For half an hour I bore the brunt of their juvenile humour quietly, my fingers playing with the *mala* beads around my neck, having fixed a plastic smile

on my face but I was very happy when they got tired of me and started preying on another poor sod who had just walked in.

It dawned on me then that a pub was not the ideal location to practice my newfound piety, especially since the re-entry was still so recent. In any case it was obvious the man I had become after the ashram no longer fitted in with the people I used to be with, and the places I used to frequent. Not a single one of them in the pub would have given a shit about my spiritual experience, or my brand new clarity or conviction. It would appear that I had, once again, painted myself into another lonely corner.

A REASON FOR LIVING

And so I kept my inner circle small. There was mostly work, and then time spent at home, reading or watching DVDs and the regular visits to the ashram for moral support. I really don't remember ever being so focused or self-contained in my life. But it was really about survival. I felt under siege from the world around me and I was building a sort of fortification using all the elements that seemed to work in my life: the business, my friendship with Made and Ngurah, and my new creed. Creed? It wasn't as if I had embraced a new kind of faith or anything. It was just a way of coping. Of dealing with the bits in my personality which were dysfunctional. Like drinking way too much for my poor liver. Or taking too much of the assortment of drugs that helped me party or mellow out. Or sleeping around with those dodgy females whom I wouldn't be caught dead with in the harsh glare of the day. Keeping to my inner circle made me a better person. It made me a man who could function better. Someone I could respect.

Or was it really just a crutch? Let me tell you, living in this

much-proclaimed 'paradise' as an almost-ascetic has been quite a feat. A real test of willpower and discipline. Just drive by the beaches of Kuta and you'd run smack into a blonde, tanned bikini-clad surfer girl strutting down the street, tits and arse half hanging out, challenging you to stick to your resolve. It's enough to make a grown man cry. Or maybe you decide to drop by one of the clubs along the Double Six strip and there you'll have a head-on (or should I say, hard-on) collision with a group of wild girls on holiday, just looking for a laugh and a tickle and a whole lot of trouble. Just thinking of all the temptations of the flesh made me quiver. At least this way I would be buffered. Protected.

Some of my friends didn't care for that kind of protection. They were worried I was going through a nervous breakdown. Like my friend Dale who appeared at my house unannounced as I was watching a movie on DVD.

'Don't you know how to answer your calls anymore? What's the problem, matey? You're too holy to pick up the bloody phone?' he asked as he plonked his substantial girth right on the very sofa that I was reclining on. I was caught unawares and could only grin like an idiot.

'So this is where you've been hiding. Do you even go into work anymore or do you just stay at home and chant your mantras or whatever it is you religious acolytes do?' he pushed on.

'I'm okay, really. Just needed some time away from the bar scene. Wanted to have some time to myself, you can understand …' I mumbled as I tried to disentangle my left leg, which was partly pinned under his sweaty, expansive bottom.

'Okay, good. You haven't lost the plot completely then … So, where's my bloody beer? Have you forgotten how to be a host?

Chop-chop!!!' he barked. I almost ran to the kitchen and then I remembered as I opened the fridge. Calamity. I had no beer. I had stopped drinking alcohol.

Suffice to say Dale was not very pleased with my offer of ginger ale. He burst out, red-faced, with an apoplectic: 'You're a bloody useless excuse for a human being.' And with that verdict I was dead to him. He left my house without as much as a backward glance. In all the years I have known him, I had never seen Dale move his corpulent form with as much speed as he did that day.

*   *   *

As the months passed, I gained more confidence in my new identity. The 'wanker in white' had finally found his reason for living. I can't say I was much happier but I can say there weren't any more crazy emotional dramas in my life. I was on an even keel. For a brief moment, that is, until an honourable, well-connected businessman from the big island decided he was going to build a nightclub right near my ashram.

From the balcony at the ashram, we all watched with interest the construction of the two-storey club. As is the way of the ashram, not one word of displeasure or dismay was expressed whenever we looked on to the den of iniquity as it steadily gained form. Only once did I notice the Head Guru of the ashram shake his head wordlessly as he contemplated the future that lay ahead with the nightclub in the neighbourhood. Were our concerns justified? Well, as fate would have it, all our niggling doubts and fears were warranted.

It wasn't as if the people in the neighbourhood were opposed

to strangers in their midst. Quite the contrary. They were already used to the odd assortment of 'spiritual guests' from all around the world whom would stay at the ashram for as long as a week to a year. Then some bright spark decided he would invest in a vegetarian café a few doors down which proved to be so profitable that six months later, another entrepreneurial couple opened a vegetarian bakery, and following that someone else decided on a juice bar. And after, a local man opened a small *warung* which sold vegetarian Indonesian food (loads of spicy *tempe* and mounds of *gado-gado*). So this neighbourhood had grown accustomed to seeing ashram disciples, hippies, vegetarian diners and curiosity-seekers; outsiders whom were all looking for a break from the ubiquitous *babi guling* and the other tourist traps that lined the crowded beaches and other holiday-making locations on the island.

That was how the ashram had been the unwitting catalyst for the neighbourhood becoming trendy and hip and congested. More and more people started to pour into the area, their cars lined up bumper to bumper on the roads and parked all along the side of the roads. For the large part, the foreigners were there to be served (food and drinks, packaged spirituality) and the locals were there in search of jobs. I watched these developments with some amusement but for some reason the nightclub really bothered me. Ironic really because only six months ago I would have gone to such a place without any qualms.

It was obvious the people who frequented the place didn't quite fit in with the 'soul' of our locale. For one, the music they played would go on till the wee hours of the morning. It was the migraine-inducing and gut-churning *thump-thump-thump*

electronica sounds of techno or house music. A new type of clientele appeared: mini-skirted and halter-topped local and foreign women, already inebriated, would walk in late into the night, the men just as dodgy in their tight pants and singlet tops proudly showing off tattoos and muscles. Soon there was talk that one could get a number of drugs at the place in addition to the boys and girls for hire. Then fights started to break out almost every night. Each morning broken bottles could be found on the road leading to the club.

The residents and business owners formed a committee in order to handle the problem of the nightclub. It was decided that three representatives would meet with the manager and the owner of the club to discuss the problem of noise, brawling and the rumours of drugs and prostitution on its premises. The meeting went well and the manager and one of the owners (apparently the place was owned by one local and three foreign partners) agreed to look into the problem areas. For three days the place shut at 11 pm and the noise levels were well within tolerable limits. There were no fights for one week after the meeting, and in fact the club had hired some muscle of their own to keep trouble-makers in line. So everything was back to normal. But for just one week.

After that week, the club stayed open past midnight. The sound levels were still bearable at first but then we noticed that the music was still on after midnight. Soon the noise was back to what it was before the meeting. The broken bottles re-appeared two weeks after the meeting. Fortunately there were no fights as the club bouncers were still keeping the peace at the place. But after three weeks the all hired brawn was no longer to be seen. And then a few nights later, there was terrific fracas involving five

men and one of them almost died due to serious head injuries. The police and ambulance were there and there was even a fire engine as a blaze had broken out because one of the clashing geniuses decided to lob a Molotov cocktail into the patio of the club. Pandemonium.

Our ashram group was relieved when we heard the police had ordered the club to be shut down. And then someone had put up a sign that said the club would be closed indefinitely. Our prayers had been answered. For one whole month life on the street was tranquil. Even the traffic and parking problem seemed to have subsided. The general mood was mellow in the neighbourhood and I was very contented with life. That is until I saw her again.

I was taking a breather at the balcony of the ashram after a marathon group-meditation session. And there she was at the burnt-out patio of the club. I was having trouble catching my breath. She was jotting down something in a small notebook. Beside her was an effeminate man dressed in a tight red plaid patterned T-shirt and an even tighter pair of jeans holding a measuring tape and a clipboard. She had changed; there was something even more aloof about her demeanour. Or was it her new posh hairstyle, with those blonde highlights, and swanky designer clothes that created an instant wall between her and the rest of us mere mortals?

I don't even remember leaving the ashram and walking towards the club but the next thing I knew I was right at its main gate. And then I couldn't move. What would I say to her? What if she just snubbed me? After all, she did leave me without a parting word. I was just about to walk away when I heard her voice calling out my name.

'Scott. Is that you?' She walked towards me.

I nodded, trying on an unsteady smile as I kept nodding because I didn't trust myself to say anything.

'I would never expect to meet you here. You look good. You're skinny now but you look good.' Her hand was on my arm but it felt as if someone was choking me. She tightened her clutch on my arm and all I could see was her big diamond ring sparkling brightly in the morning sun – it was probably a three-carat gemstone. I wanted to run to the drain and throw up the *lassi* I had for breakfast.

'What are you doing here?' I blurted out, shaking her hand off my arm gently.

'The nightclub needs a major renovation and I'm in charge. My husband is one of the owners,' she smiled. *Her husband.*

'Oh … so what are you going to do with the place?' The last thing I wanted to do was to chat about her stupid tycoon husband. 'Is it still a club or are you going to turn it into a restaurant or something?' I asked hopefully.

'Well, because the nightclub has caused so much trouble we thought we'd turn it into a private club. Only for members. People like my husband and his friends. A place where they can have a nice meal, listen to good music and maybe get a foot or back massage in one corner.'

I nodded in approval but my heart was filled with pure hatred. A bunch of rich fat old bastards coming to this neighbourhood with their Mercedes and BMWs and lording it up. I could just see them throwing their weight around because they had the money and status. Worst of all one of them was *the* rich fat old bastard who took her away from me.

I told her about the ashram and how I was a regular there. Then I made some excuse about how I was late for a meditation session and I left her abruptly. She gave me her business card before I left but I didn't even look at it. As soon as I was out of her sight I tore it and threw it into a heap of rubbish that the ashram's gardener was about to burn. I hated what she had become. But most of all I hated that the mere sight of her made me a seething mess.

THE PURIFICATION

She called me twice after we met at the club. The first time she tried the office but I told Ngurah to say that I was out on an appointment with a client. The second time she called me on my mobile phone. Her number wasn't displayed so I had no way of knowing that it was her. I answered and she sounded very happy to hear my voice. She said that she was so glad that we had met and she hoped that we could remain friends despite all that had happened. I kept silent as she blabbered on nervously. She said that we should meet, perhaps for dinner. There was no mention of her husband. What a cliché. She had become one of those neglected and bored rich men's wives hoping to find some solace in a former lover's arms. A real fucking joke.

I tossed and turned in bed that night. I felt as if I was coming down with something: my head hurt, I felt feverish and nauseated. Even if I did find a way to avoid having dinner with her I would still run the risk of bumping into her each time I went to the ashram. I didn't want to be with her, I didn't want to become weak and lost again. She was poison to me. I knew I had to act fast. But I had no idea what to do.

I burnt incense again that night. I tried to meditate but my breathing was too shallow and my mind too distracted to keep my focus. I just sat and watched the red glow of the incense sticks burn down to the wood. And the thought came to me, like a torch-light cutting through a jet-black night.

* * *

The night sky was an intense orange-crimson from the inferno. Fortunately the night watchman escaped unscathed. The flames raged on for three days. The fire engine tried to put it out but the blaze was too big to control. In the end the club was reduced to a black pile of charred rubble. The club was closed for good. And then we heard the news the owners were going to lease the land out to build a spiritual spa. Whatever that meant I did not really know but it certainly sounded more suitable for the neighbourhood than a member's club for a group of degenerate rich old men.

I never saw her or heard from her again. It was almost as if she had died in the fire that night. But I knew that she was alive and well, and beyond my reach. She was back at her husband's side and she was probably busy organising dinner parties or charity balls or whatever it is that rich men's wives do to pass the time. I prayed that our paths would never cross again.

I'd like to believe that what I did was for the greater good of the community. I tell myself that I had helped to keep the spirit of the neighbourhood true to itself. The last thing we needed was a group of strangers whom were disrespectful and insensitive to our values. After all we had tried the diplomatic way with them and

it got us nowhere.

After the fire, it was decided that any new business proposals would be vetted by the *banjar*, the neighbourhood association, before it could operate in the area. The ashram people nominated me to represent them at the *banjar* meetings. They said I would be the most appropriate representative because I was a businessman and I could be firm during any discussions especially if these involved any foreigners. I felt honoured by their trust. I had been thinking of selling my home in Canggu and building a new one in this neighbourhood so that I can be close to the ashram and perhaps take on a more active role in its day-to-day affairs.

So here I am living a life that is so different from anything that I had ever imagined. I'm amazed that for the first time in my life I can honestly say I'm leading an honourable life, surrounded by honourable people. But through it all, I have never, ever thought of Bali as paradise on earth ...

THE STUDIO

He was tired. Bone tired. Endless days just soaking in this tropical lassitude, immersed in wanton pleasures, absorbed in aesthetic amusements – a series of never-ending sensory indulgences in his green, green Eden. All that was required of him was to wake up, paint, eat, get drunk and have rowdy sex with his new young insatiable wife, Dewi. Or wake up, have rowdy sex, paint, get drunk and then eat. In whatever order he chose.

For in this, his very own kingdom, routines and duties were frowned upon. He was the master of his own destiny. Or so his friends thought. The ones he left behind. Those friends burning green with envy, the ones still chasing endless deadlines at work; encumbered with second or third mortgages: if they were lucky, for their second or third homes; saving for their kids' college education; another car loan for the latest SUV model or if the wife permitted, a hot Italian sports car or a motorbike; recovering from yet another bout of ulcer; taking medication to stave off an inevitable angioplasty or God forbid, a triple bypass. All the wonderful privileges of progress. Of success. From that perfect life he left behind. The paragon of a wife he left behind. The wholesome kids he left behind.

His friends would come to visit him at the studio, a quick detour while on their five-star Bali holiday, their wives having pledged allegiance to his own abandoned spouse would stay back

at the hotel, opting instead for the half-day deluxe spa experience. He could picture the wives with their pinched, pale faces, nostrils flaring, thin lips pursed in sour disapproval. 'Talk some sense into him, would ya? 'Kelly is still hoping he'll come back, y'know?' 'There are less damaging ways to deal with mid-life crisis, for Christ's sake!' 'Who does he think he is, some kind of American Gauguin?' 'Shacking up with some girl, young enough to be his daughter! Isn't he ashamed? Poor, poor Kelly!'

And so their husbands would come to see him, at first looking guilty and sheepish, but then the dam would break and they would trip all over themselves congratulating him, cheering him on for having the guts to grab for himself a life they only dreamed about but had no balls going after. He would break out a six-pack of Bintang beer together with some local moonshine they called '*arak*' which he would serve as shooters right in the middle of his bare studio. He would tell them of all his adventures since he left the Midwest. Since he abandoned his brilliant career as the Group Creative Director of the multi-national advertising agency, leaving his home in the dead of night with all his worldly belongings in a backpack and clad in a pair of faded old jeans and an even older t-shirt with The Clash emblazoned on the front.

They would get drunk, exchange ribald tales about their escapades with forbidden women (real or imagined), talk about work a bit, and then they would grill him about his life. His new life in paradise. A nubile exotic beauty at his side. He was doing something he loved (painting) and doing it well. He would regale them with these tales because he knew this was expected of him. Like a performer he knew he had to keep his energy levels up for his audience. He could never display the weariness, the

creeping sense of finality and decay laid bare by this beautiful island. All made too clear by the strong, sensual young Balinese bodies, exhibited without shame during their communal baths by the river, and then even more so by the decrepit old ones – once belonging to sturdy farmers, their fecund wives – now bent over and shrivelled from years of toil, now pacing the village roads aimless and alone, just waiting to die.

Once, he had tried to imagine what it would be like to climb into one of those fancy funeral pyres, the ones the locals made such a fuss about. He thought of setting himself ablaze. Have the flames licking at his skin, burning into his flesh. What would that be like? He shivered. Yeah, and then what? Rise like the phoenix, reborn? No. He was just being stupid, mostly feeling dumb and numb, and his paintings were beginning to show for it. The fervour was dissipating. The joy of discovery was all about done. It was just mostly the same thing day in and day out. A holding pattern. At least the sex was still quite good. Although lately he had been having some trouble getting it up for Dewi. But Agung his friend at the *warung* nearby gave him a herbal concoction, some *jamu*, to help him stay erect long enough to satisfy his tasty, greedy Dewi.

And so his friends came and went. Their visits became much like a class trip to the zoo. They'd leave some goodies from civilisation, sometimes it was the best single malt scotch their money could buy or some of those contraband Cuban cigars he loved so much. He was glad to see them leave because frankly, he was getting weary of the act. And he knew they were tired too, of being envious, resentful middle-aged men counting down their days. But lately, the silence they left behind was overwhelming.

More than once, he had to catch his breath as he spent hours staring into an empty canvas, or just lying in the middle of his big, bare studio. No amount of blandishments from the art critics could cheer him up. And no amount of romps in the sack with his hot, limber Dewi could lighten his mood.

Ahhh ... Sweet, sweet Dewi. He met her one sunny afternoon in a gallery in Pengosekan. They were the only two people there. She was a fresh-faced young beauty with a curvy, compact body built for sex. She said she was a sculptor but to make ends meet she now worked as a photographer's assistant. She wanted to show him her work so that he could give her his honest opinion on her potential. He agreed but all he really wanted was for her to show him her beautiful body. He wanted her to show him the full length of her glowing, smooth as silk brown skin. He wanted to paint her nude but making such a request would have been conduct unbecoming of a fellow artist.

But the Gods must have been smiling on him, because she was desperately looking for a mentor, a father figure and for a time he was quite willing to play the role. And so, restraining his baser instincts and quelling his innumerable hard-ons when she was around, they began to spend a lot of time together. Soon Dewi was staying away from her *kos*, that dingy armpit of a boarding room and she began spending nights at his studio. She insisted on sleeping on the thin mattress on the floor while he slept on his comfortable kapok-filled double bed in a separate room, tossing and turning, conflicted between desire and well, desire ... Not wanting to scare her away for good, he didn't dare make a move.

He did his best paintings in those days. Dewi would watch silently, fussing over him every so often to drink some coffee or

have a meal. In turn, at the end of the day, he would treat her to a nice dinner at one of the tourist joints or to some beer at one of the friendly drinking holes where all the expats and exiles in town flocked to. Sometimes he would drive her all the way to Kuta to take her shopping and he would let her splurge on a new dress, cosmetics, shoes – anything she wanted with all the money he got from yet another sale of his paintings in Jakarta, New York or London.

He didn't know what it was, maybe it was the new stuff that she wore or being in his company on regular basis, but Dewi was becoming more confident and more outspoken. Heck, she was becoming more beautiful with each passing day. The other old *bule* hounds in town were sniffing around her but she stayed loyal to him, his sweet Dewi. Sometimes they would stay in and she would cook for him, one of those combustible *sambal* dishes (which always gave him heartburn) with some stir-fried vegetables and rice. It was all very intimate. Sitting on the floor of his studio, the food all laid out on the mat in front of them with flickering candlelight for effect, they were like ship-wrecked lovers on some tropical hideaway. But even up till then, the marooned couple weren't doing the deed. They didn't even kiss, merely some safe hand-holding and even safer back rubs that Dewi doled out after a long day of painting.

It was during *purnama*, he remembered because the locals observed each full moon with special prayers at the temple and he remembered sitting in the *bale* outside smoking a big fat stogie, watching the women go by, graceful and proud in their colourful lace *kebaya*s, carrying multi-tiered fruit, flower and confectionery offerings on their heads. He heaved a big sigh as they passed: they

looked so alluring and yet untouchable, they made him feel old and so foreign to this land. He didn't feel like having dinner that night, just a liquid diet consisting of three big bottles of beer and then he was ready to hit the sack. Dewi was somewhere in the house or maybe she was out visiting some of her old friends from art school; he couldn't really remember.

He fell into a deep dreamless slumber as soon as his head touched the pillow. But at some point during the night, he remembered waking up because it was so hot. The air in the room was unbearably still and the sheets around him were drenched from his sweat. He was sitting up in bed when he groggily made out the figure by the open door. It was Dewi. Her hair was damp and she was clad in a sarong tied at her chest – she looked like she had just taken a bath. She called out his name softly and she walked to the bed. When she was just a few steps from it, she let her sarong loose from the fold above her breasts and it fell down, landing softly around her ankles. And there she was in all her naked glory. The moonlight that reflected off her gleaming skin gave her an ethereal glow.

The combined effect of the booze and the heat made him slow to react. Dewi slid onto the bed and without hesitation she kissed him open-mouthed, again and again. She kicked away the sheets and climbed on top of him and touching him, caressing him until he was deep inside her. But truth be told, she was doing most of the work and by her moves there was no doubt that she knew what she was doing. It didn't take him long to get into her rhythm. She was assertive about getting the pleasure she wanted and he gladly acquiesced. He could barely keep the stupid ass grin from his face. There she was, on top of him, her endless silky

smooth brown skin melding into his, her hot body all his to touch, to kiss, to taste.

So yes, the sex was still good even after five years. But someone should have told him that even in paradise there was a time limit on passion. With the sexual tension all gone, his paintings took on a more placid mood. There was so much less of the anger and frustration to motivate the long, manic sessions of painting, of venting. Obsessive sessions which once produced some of his finest work, work that amazed even him because he didn't think he had it in him. Yup, those days were done. He was a contented man now: well fed, well taken care of, well sexed up. He was just one very lucky bastard.

His paintings were selling well in Jakarta and abroad and even right here in town. His decision to renovate one of the rooms in the front into a small gallery had paid off. Many people had begun to drop in to look and sometimes to buy. Dewi would help him out on from time to time but he was quite happy for the occasional distraction. Sometimes he would meet a visitor with whom he would chat the whole afternoon away. Sharing a cold beer and catching up on gossip and news from the frantic world he had left behind. He had no real complaints. Life was generally quite good.

So why was he getting that feeling again? That ugly sensation in the pit of his stomach. Sometimes it felt like perpetual acid reflux. And what was with the breathlessness? He was also having some difficulty sleeping, maybe it was because Dewi was a rough sleeper, the kind that tossed and turned throughout the night and hogged most of the bed. But he knew there was probably something more. Like that time he woke up in the middle of the

night and gave himself a fright. He couldn't remember where he was and what he was doing holding the young brown-skinned girl in his arms. His skin looked so white, so old and mottled next to hers, so taut and radiant with youth. He was mortified.

Fortunately the nocturnal panic attacks weren't a constant companion. Most of his days went by uneventfully, according to the gentle rhythms of the land. Life was pretty much centred on the same activities, with differing permutations of schedules and jumbled regularity to keep boredom and routine at bay. He had started downing Agung's *jamu* drinks on daily basis. He told himself it was just as an energy booster but it was really something he needed for his flagging libido. It wasn't that Dewi had ceased to be sexually attractive to him but he knew that something was definitely amiss.

The two things he could always count on in the past it were his sexual drive and his passion for his work. It was intertwined. His various sexual conquests were widely known at his previous job. The men used to make jokes and placed bets on it. But even the thrill of his conquests lost their lustre after awhile, especially when emotions and romance started to mar the beautiful simplicity of it all. There was always some messy fall-out. After a time there were always tears, threats, ugly recriminations. Women. They would always be his downfall. And so for a time he had exhausted himself back to a state of monogamy. He returned to the safety of being a husband, and so he became all Kelly's. He played the attentive Dad to the kids. At the office, he kept his focus solely on the work. For two long years and then he could play the role no longer. And so he made the decision to leave.

Now he was all Dewi's. He was her toy. Her willing, breathing,

living vibrator. And yet there was a void that she couldn't fill, no matter how attentive, how thorough her ministrations in and out of bed. It wasn't that she was stupid or anything, she was definitely more intelligent that most of the women he'd ever been with before or during his marriage to Kelly. But increased familiarity and the growing expectations of a relationship made it all much more of an effort. For one, there was his inexplicable jealousy. This was new to him.

These days every time she left the house wearing something nice, her body perfumed, he suspected her of cheating on him. He suspected her of going out for a tryst with some local stud who had the stamina of a thoroughbred. It was crazy. But was he? It had happened here before. Someone's woman running off with one of these testosterone-driven young guys. Yes, he knew them well. All smiles and oozing charm with the ladies, muscles rippling, hard-ons in 0.03 seconds or less. They were like walking penises. Why was he thinking like this? Maybe he was just going crazy. Just plain old and crazy.

But he knew in his gut that if there was anyone who was more likely to cheat it would be him. He had been thinking and fantasising about other women a lot more than usual lately. Wondering what it would be like to have them in his bed. Heck, to have them right here in the middle of the studio. Going at it like those skinny, mangy Balinese dogs in heat. There was that young hippie French girl who had been coming to the studio quite a lot lately. Auburn hair cascading almost down to her waist, grey green eyes, pale golden skin with just a faint trace of freckles, always braless with pert breasts and impudent nipples that stuck right through her T-shirt. He knew all the come-on signals. The

subtle body language, the semantics of lust half hidden in her broken English. Yes, he could read them well after mastering it for over thirty years.

But he didn't have the energy to follow through. Not this time. He was intrigued but more than anything he was just weary. The many assignations of his past had taken its toll. The frenzied and forbidden fornication that was once his staple had lost its appeal. The reality of it was just too damned inconvenient for him at his age. He sighed in deep resignation. Oh, but he could still dream. The sensation of it all remains as palpable as the taste of a sweet juicy, runny fruit on a hot summer's day. So here he was, left with the consuming familiarity of sex with Dewi. Yes, it was a bit of an effort these days but it would just have to do. Until he could no longer bear it all. He knew he was just tired. Bone tired.

EXILE

She never wanted to be the person she had become. An anxious and overweight housewife, waking up each day begrudging the life that fate had dished out to her. She waited every day for her husband to come home a changed man: to tell her that she meant something to him, to tell her that she was still very much loved and desired. His words would ring in her head for hours, days, weeks after he uttered them.

'Why is this soup so tasteless – haven't you seen my mother cook this hundreds of times?'

'Do you have to wear that dress? You look like somebody's maid.'

'Do you think you can find something better to do with your time instead of just watching those soap operas and eating the whole day? You're getting so fat already.'

'Isn't it obvious? Why do you have to be so stupid?'

But he remained the same. He would come home seething as he always did. Angry at something someone at the office did or didn't do. Angry at how the stock market performed. Angry at how an investor was playing games in negotiations. Angry at the way the lazy, good-for-nothing mechanic repaired his Mercedes. Angry at the way the government was running the country. But most of all knew he was angry that she was in his life: unhappy and dependent. He was resentful and bitter that he wasn't blessed

with a more suitable wife: a stylish, svelte creature that he could parade at all the country clubs, the dinners that he was invited to at all the exclusive restaurants; someone who could keep him aroused in bed, night after night. It was a cruel twist of fate that God had granted him wealth but short-changed him on his spouse and children: sullen, stupid creatures that drained his resources and patience.

But this story is about her. And how everything changed in a dizzying moment of anger that swept her life along a wave of transformation. She would have liked to say it was a path of redemption but that would be too premature. After all there was so much in her life that was still so murky and uncharted that she sometimes felt she was treading deep waters, half-submerged. Breathing and drowning in equal measure. But it was a new life and she was very slowly learning how to leave the past behind.

It was Angela who sowed the first seeds of change. One morning she came downstairs teary-eyed and announced that she had to quit and return to the Philippines immediately. After ten years of employment this news was startling. Her mother had died of a heart attack and there was no one to look after her own sons at home. Angela joined the household when Ming, her daughter was only three. She was having violent arguments with her husband daily – almost anything could trigger these and Ming cowered away from her, still sensing the residual anger and bitterness from those altercations. She couldn't cope with keeping their new condo spotlessly clean as her husband liked it to be, cooking all the meals according to his exacting demands and looking after her emotionally distant daughter. She felt as if she was teetering on a precipice. Out of control and out of options.

Angela was a saviour.

With her calm disposition and efficient manner, Angela quickly and easily earned respect from her family. She also had a nursing degree which made her feel safe should any medical emergencies arise at home. Her daughter became attached to Angela's affectionate but firm ministrations. And more importantly Angela's very presence made her husband and her reticent about fighting. They felt compelled to be civil and courteous with one another for fear that Angela would judge them to be ill-bred people, or worse, inadequate parents. Slowly this uneasy detente became an all-out truce. And soon relations were cordial enough for them to conceive another child.

Their son, Sam, was born exactly nine and a half months after Angela's arrival. His presence, the much sought-after male scion, allowed her to enjoy the spill-over of her husband's affections. He became gentle and considerate towards her. He even bought her an expensive diamond tennis bracelet for her efforts at producing a male heir. He doted on his son, showering him with expensive toys and clothes. The boy was his daily balm – the dark mood he carried over from the office would dissipate as soon as he carried his son in his arms. But this was not to last for long. Sam had a sensitive soul, and he clung to Angela and her every chance he could, hungry for tenderness and reassurance. This quality earned him disfavour with his father. Her husband accused them of coddling Sam too much and turning him into a mama's boy.

The more her husband tried to mould their son into the kind of boy he deemed worthy of his surname, the more Sam pulled away from his father. He would hide in the kitchen quietly each time he heard his father come through the front door at the end

of each day. He cowered each time his father scolded him for acting like a sissy: for not wanting to play football or rough-house with the other boisterous children in the neighbourhood. Instead he would crawl silently under the table where he would scribble countless pictures of dinosaurs and action heroes. His father's overt displeasure fizzled into quiet disapproval and then resigned disappointment. He distanced himself from the boy, preferring instead to while away his leisure hours at the golf course.

She watched as Ming and Sam grew up, tiptoeing around their father. They received their expensive gifts from him but not much else. His life revolved around the intricacies of making more money and making the best deals with business partners local and foreign. His temperament was as volatile as the stock market. She even learnt to monitor the market so that she could gauge what his mood would be like when he got home. But there were always other variables at play, so even if the market was performing bullishly that day he could still very well be in foul mood. She had begun to feel like a soothsayer trying to tell the future by reading the viscera of animals – a messy endeavour that sometimes foretold events with great accuracy, but most of the time, the readings were plainly wrong.

And so the old walls came up again – her husband immersed himself in his other life, with marathon work days – twelve hours and above; afterwards, entertaining clients over dinner and drinks in dark, smoky lounges where the supple hostesses were obliging creatures, and then weekend getaways that sometimes took him off to golf courses in the region and a host of unknown social engagements with his friends – other over-achieving business executives who spoke in a language that was all about the

performance of the stock market and never-ending deals that were aimed at earning them millions of dollars. They cheered each other on and competed with each other in business and in sports, like over-aged members of a college fraternity where everyone else around them was peripheral. Their wives, their children were all hapless satellites orbiting endlessly around them.

She was the one who had slipped off orbit onto a dangerous trajectory. A mishap that stemmed from so many nights of falling asleep alone, hating her husband even as much as she missed him, hating herself for not being able to give voice to her growing frustration and anger. Angela was no longer around to act as their moral compass, as the unofficial referee for their bitter disputes, both spoken and unspoken. And then the agent delivered a young girl named Ayu to replace Angela. A pretty, waif of a thing whom she suspected was just fresh out of the village.

Ayu, who couldn't even speak English, was constantly bewildered by all the electrical appliances in the house and perpetually shocked at the amount of food that was consumed and thrown away after each meal. She ate sparingly and worked long hours without complaint: much like an ox, with great strength but little finesse. On her very first day at the house, she broke two bone china teacups. These were part of a set, a precious wedding gift from a dear aunt now dead. Ayu cried, sobbing uncontrollably when she was telling her about the cups. She was livid but her anger quickly dissipated when she realised that Ayu was genuinely stricken with remorse and fear.

She was continually exasperated with the girl in the first few weeks but Ayu seemed so pathetic and helpless that it aroused her compassion. And she was adamant her husband would not

have the satisfaction of seeing her crumble at this latest domestic challenge. He would certainly interpret it as yet another way she fell short as the ideal and capable wife. And so she put all her energy towards turning Ayu into an acceptable housekeeper. She taught Ayu how to operate all the electrical appliances with increasing ease; the girl even learnt to cook a few of the family's favourite dishes. Ming and Sam were taken by her gentle ways with them and, in turn, Ayu gave in to their every demand with patience and affection.

For her part, she was happy that her universe was slowly returning to its former equilibrium. But there were still some areas that were a source of concern. She was frankly dismayed at the amount of Indonesian language that was creeping into her children's daily speech. Because of Ayu's limited English vocabulary they were all forced to speak the language that she felt was beneath them but there was really no other choice in the matter. And the girl just didn't know how to clean like Angela. When Angela was in the midst of her rigorous cleaning sessions, the condo would look like a mini-hurricane had hit it. Stripped down to a pair of faded, baggy shorts and T-shirt, she would push all the chairs and tables to the side, the rugs and carpets were rolled up on top of the furniture, with TVs, hi-fis, and computers all unplugged and heaped on tables. But afterwards the floors would gleam from her efforts. With Angela it always looked like one could confidently eat straight off the floors. With Ayu it was a hit-or-miss situation. There were days when her cleaning was adequate but when Ayu had to cater to the children's whims and demands then the standards would suffer. Dishes would start piling up in the sink, the floors would be clean enough but there would be some spots

which were obviously done quite haphazardly. Sometimes the laundry was left in heaps in the utility room: the piles to be ironed and the one to be washed hardly distinguishable.

During these times, she would quietly take up the slack, mopping the floors over again and polishing them until they shone. She would grit her teeth while quietly doing the dishes and putting the wash in the machine. Her husband would be the first to notice any shortcomings in the quality of cleaning. It was yet another way he maintained control over the household and wielded his power over her. And as much as she hated herself for it, this was a pattern to which she had helplessly succumbed very early in their marriage.

Her husband was taciturn with Ayu, preferring instead to watch her quietly as she worked around the house or attended to the children. The girl seemed to sense his disapproval and she kept a safe distance from him; gingerly going about her chores when he was around. Once in a while, in a low voice he would warn her that Ayu was to be watched very closely and that she should never be left alone in the house. 'These people can't be trusted you know; she'll bring her boyfriend and his gang into the house and they'll rob us.'

It was useless trying to tell him that Ayu didn't have a boyfriend; he would just tell her that she didn't know anything. 'Just listen to me lah. You're too busy reading your silly gossip magazines and watching TV to notice anything.' The truth was the girl was too scared to venture out of the condominium. Outside the people were always in a hurry and unsmiling, their cars – miles and miles of them – were always zooming by at breakneck speeds, the street signs and billboards were all in languages alien

to her. Sensory overload. She didn't even have any friends to chat with, only the occasional phone call to her mother back home, loud conversations in an unknown Indonesian dialect that would always end up in tears. Then Ayu would be sombre for days, enervated. It was as if all her good cheer and youthful energy had been transmitted back to her village and all that was left was this shell of a girl.

But it wasn't too long after her husband's cautionary words that Ayu found herself as the object of a young man's affections. The dark wiry Indonesian boy wore extremely tight jeans and snug T-shirts at least two sizes too small. His shoulder length hair was always greased back neatly. He was working at a construction site not far from the condominium. He had caught a glimpse of Ayu one afternoon as she was accompanying Ming from the supermarket. He was instantly smitten. He would wait at the guardhouse day after day, hoping for Ayu to emerge. She was frightened of him at first but his persistence finally paid off. She was homesick and the boy provided a ready link to the life and the people she sorely missed.

She watched closely as Ayu seemed to blossom from the boy's attentions. The girl's moods were certainly more buoyant since he had appeared and there was renewed vigour to her work around the house. But she couldn't say a word to her husband as he would definitely demand that Ayu be fired immediately. That would leave her in an even more precarious position, having to do all the housework by herself whilst having to put up with her husband's derision. She could imagine what he would say: 'Didn't I tell you not to trust these people? For all you know she's been bringing the boy into our house, into our bed!' She would have

to put herself through the process of screening new applicants again, training yet another novice – another village debutante and learning to trust another stranger in her home. It was an untenable situation and she had no stomach for yet another upheaval in her world. And so she abetted in their growing love affair, all the time praying that Ayu would not do anything to violate her trust and leave her vulnerable to even more of her husband's anger and scorn.

The boy had a transforming effect on Ayu. Overnight it seemed she had become this confident well-groomed girl who worked efficiently at all her chores. Gone were the shapeless shirts and shorts, she now chose her clothes more carefully, even spending some money to buy new ones which were brightly coloured and form-fitting. And when the housework was done she would ask for permission to go for a walk and she would be gone for at least two hours.

A passionate lovers' tryst in some secluded corner or just an innocent walk? She had no way of knowing what Ayu was really up to with her boyfriend. She couldn't advise the girl about the dangers of unprotected sex: her command of the Indonesian language was just too limited for her to broach the subject with Ayu. And anyway the whole thing was just too unsavoury to consider. Here she was, night after night, hoping and waiting for her husband to reach across the bed to touch her, and night after night, nothing. He'd fall into bed and start snoring almost immediately. And then this slip of a girl comes along, straight off the boat and in a blink of an eye, she was sexually active with her construction worker. Fate had a cruel way of making all the deficits in her own life so painfully obvious.

Her husband started spending more time away from their home. He would frequently take short business trips and he would be gone for three or four days at a time. She didn't think anything about it at first but her suspicion began to grow. He was actually changing, morphing into this man she hardly knew. First, the membership at the gym. Then his clothes started getting younger. Floral shirts, tight T-shirts, designer jeans and shoes. He now opted for haircuts which were trendier than his usual barbershop style. (She didn't dare ask but she was quite certain he had even begun dyeing the grey hair on his temples with some reddish brown tint.) He had manicures on a regular basis. Then his glasses were gone, replaced by contact lenses – he was even talking about repairing his eyesight with laser surgery. Where did all this vanity come from? Another woman? Or, God forbid, another man?

Her friends advised her to hire a private investigator. One even supplied the name of a reputable firm in town. She had to know the truth before the children and she were abandoned with no money of their own to speak of. It was a worn-out cliché: a successful businessman, approaching middle-age, rediscovers his youth in the arms of a nubile temptress, leaves his family and starts a brand new one. How would Ming be able to go to university in Britain if he refused to support her education? Then there was Sam. He was still a child. He needed his father. They all needed him. She had to find out just how far-gone he was. There was much too much at stake.

It was almost a week and a half before the P.I. called her. His respectful and rather apologetic tone was ominous. He didn't divulge much over the phone but she knew that when they would

meet face-to-face, he would merely be confirming her worst fears. Her husband was having an affair. A love affair. And he may even be contemplating leaving their family for his lover. When she met the P.I., he told her that her husband's lover was a foreign national and that she had just arrived in the country about six months ago. She worked in an up-market lounge where businessmen gathered with friends or entertained their corporate clients. There was a picture of her in all her glory. A tall, willowy girl with alabaster skin. She couldn't have been more than twenty-five. She had a heart-shaped face framed by centre-parted long hair that fell below her shoulders like a cascade of black silk. She wasn't a skinny girl. The sleeveless top she wore had a plunging neckline and it was obvious that the girl had full breasts. She peered closely at the photo the P.I. had given her, putting on her reading spectacles: yes, definitely, the girl's big breasts were real and not boosted by a padded bra, she told herself quite detachedly.

She put away her glasses with a sigh and stared at the P.I. in a daze. So her husband had finally found his ideal woman. Someone he could parade in front of his other womanising friends; someone whom they could all lust after. Someone whom he just couldn't keep his hands off. Someone totally different from her. (She looked at herself in the Marks & Spencer ensemble of a plain lime green blouse and black cotton pants, and an afterthought, a necklace of black crystal beads – it shouted out: 'I'm a housewife, I have no time for fashion.') To confront him at this juncture would be foolhardy. It might force his hand and induce him to leave them even sooner than he had ever considered. She had to be smart about this. She had to do all she could to protect the interests of family. Her children's inheritance was at stake. Her

comfort and security were in jeopardy.

Three nights later her husband was at home. He was as quiet and sullen as usual but she was not going to be intimidated. She had cooked four of his favourite dishes, having slaved in the kitchen for three hours. And for a change she dressed up for dinner, wearing a brand new black silk dress she had bought at a boutique. She even sprayed on some perfume as a finishing touch. If he noticed the special effort he didn't say a word. He only raised his eyebrow when he saw the spread of food on the table and that was the extent of his acknowledgment. After all, a 'thank you' from him would have been too much of a stretch. They ate their dinner in silence as they usually did. When he was done he got up and went to the balcony, closed the sliding door from outside and he made a call on his mobile phone. His conversation lasted for nearly an hour. She assumed it was with his lover. He had become a lovelorn teenager. It made her feel nauseated but she could never show him that she was aware of his infidelity. Yes, this time it was infidelity because it didn't last a mere weekend. It was more than a tawdry hotel dalliance. He had rented an apartment for his young lover. He had even changed his appearance to please this woman. This time he was undeniably unfaithful.

It seemed that she was destined to be surrounded by people in love. Ayu certainly behaved as if she was in love. The girl took frequent breaks throughout the day to speak to the construction worker on her mobile phone. It didn't disrupt Ayu's work routine but nevertheless she found it annoying. Sometimes she could overhear Ayu's conversations with her boyfriend, she couldn't understand what they were saying but the intonations and exclamations were unmistakable. Husky, pleading, baby-

like, coy and enticing all at the same time. Yes, it was all about love. She could feel her stomach churning, the bile rising as she fought against the reflex to vomit. She chalked it up to nerves. But whatever it was, she knew it was building up inside her. Steadily. And menacingly.

The next few weeks involved frantic, covert meetings with lawyers and accountants. As a rule she distrusted them. No, perhaps disliked was more accurate a word. She always felt they condescended to women like her because they thought she was congenitally stupid. Only professionals and other people who made real money deserved their high estimation. The rest of the world, people like her, were just extras: actors in bit parts while they took centre stage running the world with their spreadsheets and their statutes. She didn't care how they looked at her and what they thought this time as long as they delivered what she needed. And what she needed was some real assurance that her future and her children's future would be safeguarded. No matter if her husband left them and decided he wanted five children with his foreign mistress.

Her husband came home only twice a week now. He didn't even bother to make any excuses about his absences. He seemed to be in a better mood each time he was home these days. Perhaps it was because he knew that the dreary existence with her and the children wasn't to be the extent of his life. He had found succour in another home, with another woman whom made him feel young and revitalised. His young lover made him feel like a man: powerful and all-knowing. There was no constant reminder of how life had fallen short of expectations. His other life was all about hope and creating something better for the future. He

would have to tell his wife, of course, that he was leaving but for now, he could, at the very least, be decent to her and the children. After all they stood to lose so much. They stood to lose him.

Her constant nausea was beginning to worry her. At first she thought it was just due to indigestion: biliousness from the stress and worry. Pregnancy was not even in the equation. Her husband had not touched her for years. The children and food had been her only comfort for years. Although lately, Ming and Sam seemed to sense that something was wrong and so they kept away from the condo as much as they could. There were extra-curricular activities, tuition classes, jaunts to the cinema and mall, and sleep-overs at their best friends' houses. Food had lost its appeal. She couldn't seem to hold her food down and all she wanted to do when she wasn't sorting out the finances and the legality of her husband's imminent departure, was to crawl into bed and sleep. And so she would sleep for hours, day and night. Waking up only when her husband (or his secretary) would call to ask what was going to be served for dinner. That question had become his code words for: 'I'm coming home tonight, so make sure that I am served good food for my kindness. And make sure that the condo is immaculate for my return.'

So they kept to this routine for almost six months. She sought solace in sleep whenever she could. Rising only when he came back, to keep up the pretence that all was well in the home and the marriage. Her children seemed to be growing up fast, but they were much more affectionate and tender with her than they had ever been in years. Ayu was still seeing her boyfriend and more than once she had caught her sneaking back into the condo just before daybreak. But she was too tired to reproach her. So far

Ayu hadn't gotten herself pregnant and she was certainly doing her very best to keep the condo in flawless condition. Which was all she could ask for because she had neither the energy nor the desire to play the role of the happy homemaker when her husband was cavorting around town with his beautiful, slim young foreign whore.

One day she was awakened from deep slumber by a telephone call from her husband's secretary (or executive assistant, as the woman preferred to be known); her husband was coming home that night. She sat on the edge of the bed, disoriented. The room was in semi-darkness, the curtains were all drawn except for a sliver of daylight. The air-conditioning was turned up almost full blast and she shivered slightly because she had kicked aside the down quilt. She felt inexplicably angry because of the momentary disorientation and discomfort. The anger simmered ever so slowly and then boiled over in a totally unexpected way. It seemed to crash through her half sedated consciousness and infuse her with a manic energy.

If his husband wanted her act like his wife tonight well that was what he would get. She changed into a clean T-shirt and pants and brushed her hair with ferocity. Then she started busying herself in the kitchen. In no time at all she was in a frenzy of peeling, chopping, dicing, blending, boiling, frying and roasting. She would cook him a feast as one would expect a good wife to do after a hard day at the office. She didn't ask for Ayu's help but the girl just stood by the side watching her quietly. Ayu had long suspected that something was amiss in this household – an absentee husband, children who skulked around their father whenever he was at home, a perpetually fatigued wife

who preferred to sleep rather than eat. But everything seemed to be under control tonight; Madam (as Ayu had been instructed to call her) seemed to be wide awake and full of energy and so Ayu quietly set the table while the food was being prepared.

She cooked six of her husband's favourite dishes with huge portions of each dish that seemed enough to feed two families. She wanted the dining table to be covered with food. She wanted him to eat until he could eat no more. She was stirring a big pot of soup – his mother's recipe but according to him, her soup was never quite as good as the old woman's and that was when the idea came. She ran to the bathroom and rummaged through a drawer looking for a small plastic vial. Eye drops. Back in the kitchen, she separated a portion of the steaming soup into a big bowl and squeezed all the contents of the vial into the bowl. She felt strangely contented. For that moment, she felt as if her life was finally coming into focus.

She didn't know if it would work but her friend Celine who used to be an air stewardess said that when there were any passengers who were particularly troublesome, the crew would spike their drinks with eye drops and the passenger would be purging the entire flight. And so she dutifully served her husband his dinner with a big bowl of soup. ('I hope you finally got it right this time. But I doubt it. Only my mother does this soup to perfection.') She watched him carefully as he finished the soup with loud slurping sounds and went on to the other dishes.

He seemed to be alright but after about fifteen minutes he grimaced slightly. And then another grimace, this time more noticeably. He suddenly got up and went to the bathroom. He was there for about twenty minutes before he reappeared. 'I don't

know what's wrong with this food. I've been having diarrhoea.' She calmly told him that since she was unscathed, it definitely wasn't the food – perhaps he had some kind of stomach flu, she had heard that there was a bug going around ... His only response was a loud groan before he ran back to the bathroom.

He spent most of the night alternating between the bathroom and the bed. He was well and truly sick. He was as helpless as a baby when he was ill. He pleaded for her tender ministrations, groaning and writhing as he tried to control the spasms that wracked his stomach. She indulged his every demand: tenderly wiping his brow with cool damp towel and preparing all the necessary medication to ease the diarrhoea and nausea. At one point she thought of spiking his drinking water with more eye drops but decided against it. She didn't want to kill him. She just wanted him to suffer. To understand what other people went through when they suffered. Like she did. But most of all she wanted him to need her. And only her.

He had to take medical leave for three days after the meal. He spent most of that time bed-ridden, enjoying all the attention and care that she heaped on him. He was a well-behaved patient, too weak to protest and relieved that she was always there to attend to him. In return she waited on him as if he had a critical illness. She plumped his cushions, gave him sponge baths and foot massages. If she was out of his sight for too long he would call for her; he needed to know that she was in the same room and only then would he nod off to sleep. His neediness planted some hope in her that their marriage could be salvaged. 'He still needs me, he still needs me, he still needs me, he still needs me.' She kept repeating the words to herself as if they were a mantra that could

ward off the dissolution of their marriage.

But he got better. And as he got better his true nature re-emerged. The man who was controlling, overly critical and selfish slowly came back to the fore. And then nothing that she did was quite the way it should be done. And when he was done complaining about the quality of the care and the food he was receiving, he started attacking her. Her hands were too rough, or too cold. She looked haggard. Why didn't she take better care of herself? Why didn't she teach the children manners? Why weren't they looking in on him? Why was she always dressed so dowdily? He was getting better. And as he regained more of his strength, he kept asking for his mobile phone. She told him she couldn't find it but on the very first night that he had taken ill, she switched it off and hid it deep under one of the sofa cushions. Out of sight and out of mind. There was no way she would allow his mistress to intrude into their home. Not when he had finally come home.

But he hadn't. The truth was he was eager to be back by his young lover's side. This home, his overweight wife, his diffident kids, even that maid who couldn't speak English irritated him inexplicably. Enraged him at times. The next morning when he got up, he asked her again if she had found his phone. She answered no. And he shouted at her. A string of abuses, ringing through the condo, shattering whatever remaining illusion of peace that she had been trying to create. 'Stupid!' 'Useless!' 'Ugly!' 'Fat! 'Incompetent!' 'Stupid!' 'Stupid!' 'Stupid!' Ayu was in the doorway of the bedroom with a breakfast tray for him. His tirade gave her a start and Ayu retreated to the kitchen in fear.

She stood by the side of the bed just listening to him, finally hearing each and every word he uttered and without a single

response, she left the room. She found Ayu in the kitchen cowering in the pantry. She calmly told her to attend to his needs that day as she would be busy. She took his car keys and she drove his Mercedes around and around the city centre aimlessly. She wished she had the courage to crash his precious car into a wall. She wished she could be part of the expensive wreckage, a mangled body to forever mark him as culpable. Guilty. As he should be feeling. But she couldn't. She just didn't have enough conviction to make him really pay. And knowing this made her hate herself even more.

She drove till the car ran out of petrol and she stopped to buy some but not wanting to go home she drove on some more, right to the city limits. She was driving on the highway when she suddenly felt so weary. She struggled to keep herself upright. All she wanted to do then was to go home and crawl into bed. She turned the car back towards the city and it was almost dark when she got home. She could see that all the lights in the condo were on. She wondered if the children were at home. She was overcome with sadness thinking of them and how they had to be witness to this farce of a marriage. This farce of a family. She and her husband had failed them.

She let herself in with her house keys, the condo was silent. The children weren't in. Ayu would have told them how she had left in the morning and they would have preferred to be anywhere else but here. Especially if their father was still around. She looked into their bedroom but he wasn't there. The bed was made, his wallet and shoes were still around, so he hadn't left yet. He was probably hanging around just to make sure his Mercedes was still in one piece. The door to Ayu's room was closed, she opened

it quietly and there they were. He was on the floor, his legs stretched out and Ayu was sitting on the bed, her hands were on his shoulders.

She heard someone make a blood-curdling sound, between a shriek and a shout in cold fury, and it took some time before she realised that the sound was coming from her throat. She didn't even remember grabbing the steam iron off the board but she did, and she started to hit him. Over and over again. Ayu was screaming at her to stop, telling her that she had got it all wrong: that she was just giving him a massage as he had requested. But she was beyond reason. Ayu tried to stop her and that was when she punched Ayu with her left hand, right in her face and with enough force to knock her back onto the bed. Unconscious. Her husband was groaning at the foot of the bed. His head was bleeding profusely.

She had two choices. Finish him off or disappear forever. Facing him after this would not be an option. He was vindictive enough to make sure she ended up in jail or a psychiatric hospital for the rest of her life. She looked at the bloodied iron and she felt queasy. She dropped it in the doorway and went to her room to pack a small suitcase. She got her passport, bank documents, all her jewellery and she called an ambulance. Then she left the condo.

* * *

It had been a year since she had left her home, her children. She wondered how they were doing but she couldn't risk calling them. Her husband – if he was still alive – might trace the call and find

out where she was. He could be quite resourceful that way. But perhaps he was just relieved; she was just one less complication in his life. He might have moved his mistress into their home by now, into her bed. She cried a lot in the first few months – thinking of Ming and Sam; thinking about how they were coping without her, and coping with their father as a regular fixture. She cried when she thought of …. She felt contrite thinking about how she might have hurt the poor girl. She didn't deserve the injury. But he was worth every leaden blow he received.

She wasn't quite sure how she ended up in Bali but that's where she had found herself. She had taken a cab to the airport and she didn't quite know where to go. Her friends in town were out of the question. New Zealand where her sister was living would have been too expensive and knowing what a dutiful wife her sister was, she would have been persuaded to go home after a week. She remembered having one blissful family holiday in Bali when the children were still very young. There was still a hint of affection for her in her husband's eyes back then. She was so happy and hopeful about the future. Everything seemed magical for the five days they were there.

She stayed at a cheap hotel in Kuta the first two weeks and then she found herself a small villa to rent in Kerobokan. It was a nondescript one-bedroom home owned by a Balinese family; it was tucked away on a narrow lane off a busy main road. There was a furniture warehouse at the street corner and a dusty little grocery shop on the other side. Across the road were paddy fields that were being overtaken by development. New homes were coming up rapidly – the grey concrete outer walls would appear almost overnight on its green edges, demarcating the little

dominions that people were creating. One day she would build her home there too. She also looked around for a business to start and she opened a small restaurant with a florist adjoining it.

She was very frugal with her money but she had to be even more prudent about her friendships. She couldn't tell anyone where she was really from. It was a lonely existence but she had a few acquaintances – the Balinese were easier for her to deal with because they were so accustomed to people from all over the world coming and going all the time. They were immensely tolerant of outsiders in their midst although they probably wondered what an Asian woman her age was doing all alone. Without any family or any real friends. Because of her social and business interactions with the Balinese, her grasp of the Indonesian language was getting very fluent. It helped to be at ease in the language – she felt that it made her less conspicuous. The other day someone thought that she was from Jakarta. How ironic that she used to think the language was never good enough for her or her family and now she was so dependent on it for her survival. She felt as if she was finally shedding her ignorance about the world: layer by layer, ever so slowly.

Once she thought she saw someone who looked a lot like Ayu. She followed the girl straight to her home – but of course, it wasn't Ayu. She wished there was some way she could make restitution for what she did to Ayu but she didn't see how she could. The local police would probably arrest her if they knew who she was. All she could do was to bide her time, remain unobtrusive and cordial with everyone. Maybe after a few years, the case back home would have been forgotten. Maybe her husband would forgive her by then. Then perhaps she could be

with her children again. That was what she was counting on. Until then, this modest new life, this discreet existence amongst strangers was her only hope.

FIVE DAYS

DAVID

David regained consciousness in a mind-numbing white haze, his first sensation was the drug-induced nausea. Gut wrenching. He felt like vomiting and defecating at the same time, if that was at all possible. He certainly felt like it was. He groaned deeply but what emerged was a feeble squeak. His body had been conspiring against him for months now. It started with the persistent cough and then chronic fatigue. The cough wasn't anything he had worried about too much; he was a smoker after all. The tiredness he chalked up to his long hours at work. Pushing forty, he knew he no longer had the stamina to withstand the pace and pressure like his younger colleagues. Then came the blood tests, MRIs and CAT scans. And his world changed.

He had asked Jill to marry him just before he found out. They had been together for five years. Five long years of ambivalence for him. Marked by the highs and the lows of being in a monogamous relationship. But things were finally making sense to him. At last he could see himself growing old with her. They had talked about having a small ceremony at home and then a long honeymoon in Bali or Fiji or Tahiti. A honeymoon and sabbatical. Bali was his first choice. Jill had never been there. He was sure she would love it.

Which was why they were here now. Not to celebrate their

marriage – the wedding was called off – but instead a send-off in style. They packed a few months' supply of medication, books, some clothes and they rented a charming little bungalow by the sea. They had been here for almost two months now. The first month was a blast. The joys of denial. They never spoke about his illness. That was the deal. Life was a holiday. Reading, talking, swimming and sunning during the day, and by night, fine dining and drinking at quaint little bistros spanning from Sanur to Seminyak. They fell into bed each night, exhausted, still laughing at some silly adventure of the day.

Then his body started rebelling. At first there were just little signs. Momentary breathlessness. Sudden immobility. The pains started with a vengeance after that. He was losing control. He even passed out twice but fortunately Jill wasn't with him those times. Thank God for the morphine-based medication. He didn't tell Jill that he had started on these because he didn't want her to worry. She was looking more like her old self lately. Laughing more. Feisty again. Happy.

She didn't look too happy now. He could vaguely make her out through the fog when the room stopped spinning and his stomach stopped churning. He gestured for the bed pan. Someone lifted him and he retched. And retched some more. Then he fell back weakly on his pillow, cold sweat on his brow. Jill came to his side. Feigning a smile on her quivering lips. 'You're going to be okay. You just need to get some rest, my darling. We've been overdoing it lately.' He nodded. And he lost consciousness again.

When he came to, a doctor was in the room. A young Balinese doctor, confident and gentle. She told him the prognosis (God, how he hated that bloody word), how much time she thought

he had left, what were his options, her prescribed medication. Somehow it was all simpler to accept because this was coming from a total stranger. It was easier to accept because he was a foreigner here. A transient. Nothing familiar and binding about the place, or the moment. No attachments. He still felt that there was a dream-like quality to the information being conveyed. Maybe because the potent painkillers were still clouding his mind. His vision was still blurry but he felt Jill's hand on his arm. Her hand was cold. Corpse-like.

Ahhh, that's how he would feel like. Cold. Dead. He was trying to remember why he wanted to die in Bali. Something about it being heaven on earth. About him not believing in the existence of heaven or hell. No afterlife. To him death was just going to be a great enduring silence. Complete darkness. Cessation of all feeling and thought. Like a solitary flame extinguished in an empty room. Oblivion. Alone. Although 'alone' would cease to hold the meaning it did for the living. He would simply be dead. End of story. He smiled.

He was in and out of his stupor for the next two days. He was finally lucid on the third. Jill was there as always. Huddled in the armchair in the corner. She was wrapped up in her pink pashmina – the one he bought for her some years ago in Bergdorf's. She looked so small and fragile, like one of those tropical flowers that would blossom for a day and die the next. He just couldn't get away from it. Dying. The end. Death. The final frontier. It was getting so fucking tiresome. He had just wanted to party until he keeled over. Then he wanted to be cremated. No dramas. Ashes to be strewn over a bright green paddy field in Tabanan, overlooking the sea. His final contribution to humanity. David, the fertiliser.

But he had a more pressing problem at hand. Jill. What was he going to do with her? All the countless other things in life he had fucked up, he didn't want Jill to be another one of his misadventures. Abandoned in a strange land. She was napping now. In her armchair. She had wrapped the pashmina wrapped around her head and upper body like an Indian bride in a saree. Alone and bereft. He wanted so much to hold her but he didn't even have the energy to take a piss. Mere breathing was an effort. God how he wished he could have a smoke now. And a cold beer. He just needed to think straight and figure out the best plan for Jill. For the both of them.

'Jill, wake up. Wake up please. I have to talk to you.'

'What's wrong? Are you in pain? Do you want me to call the nurse?' she woke up with a start, rubbing the sleep out of her eyes.

'Just listen. Don't say anything. Listen to me, please. While I'm still coherent. I want you to leave me now. Promise you'll walk out of here and just leave me alone. I can't stand to look at you anymore. I can't stomach this … this crazy … vigil.'

'Are you mad? What's all this about? I'm all you've got in Bali!' she's standing up now, her eyes lit up with anger and disbelief.

'It doesn't matter anymore. Get out of here. Do something with yourself. Go shopping. Get a massage at a spa. Get yourself a gigolo, get laid. Just anything. Leave me now.'

'For Christ's sake! You're delirious, David. How long am I supposed to do this?'

'For five days. Or till I'm gone. Whichever comes first.'

'You need me.'

'That's where you're wrong, I need nothing now.'

'Nothing?'

'Maybe my painkillers ... Just go.'

She picked up her book and magazines. Her sweater. Her backpack. She tried to touch him, to kiss him – tears streaming down her face, snot dripping out of her nose – she was bawling out loud like a child who had lost her parents at the shopping mall, but with every last bit of energy he had in reserve, he pushed her away. Please, please, he pleaded silently. And she was gone.

JILL

She really couldn't figure out if she was crying for David or for herself. It was just the thought of him alone, in pain in that small hospital room. The thought of him dying here in Bali with no family or friend by his side was just too much for her to bear. The anguish was like nothing she had ever experienced. Not even when her mother died. This was visceral. It was as if someone had taken a flying leap right into her gut.

She had resolved to see him through this. To be by his side until he was gone. To organise his cremation and then to throw his ashes to the wind. They had planned all this together. And then he says she wasn't needed anymore? When the tears and madness had subsided, when reason and clarity had crept back in, she began to understand why.

He was trying to save her from seeing the deterioration of his final days, final hours. To spare her from having that ugly memory indelibly imprinted in her mind. And understanding him so well, she knew it was a way out for himself too. He wanted to spare himself the indignity of his failing body in front of her. His damned pride. His vanity. He couldn't let her bear witness to the

messy business of his dying. It was all too repulsive. The blood, vomit, faeces, tears. His own fear. He'd rather let strangers deal with all of it. He was making her remember him as he used to be. Strong. Vital. Funny. He was making her remember for both of them because all his thoughts, his memories would soon cease to be.

She had been sitting on the veranda overlooking the beach. She was hunched up in the corner, on the floor. She had been crying for hours until her eyes could produce no more tears. They were almost swollen shut. Prizefighter's eyes. He had no right to cut her loose like this. Just like one of the many possessions he had given away before their trip. His favourite records, his CDs, his books, his cashmeres, his suits, his silk ties. His Jill.

She stumbled back into the house and fell on their bed fully clothed. She tried to remember the last time they had made love. It was all getting hazy now. It was as if her sorrow had scoured away everything they had shared together. And he wasn't even dead yet. What did he say at the hospital? Get laid? It was hard for her to imagine having another body next to hers. Another man touching her, inside her. It was inconceivable. Having sex with a stranger in this bed while he lay dying in his. It would have to be the ultimate betrayal to everything they had. Perhaps that was why he suggested it. It would be the point of no return. Not that there would be anything from their old life to go back to. David had made sure of it. Five days, he said.

Five days. And this was only the end of day one. She curled herself into a ball on David's side of the bed. She wondered how he was doing now and whether he was still in a lot of pain. She reached for the phone on the bedside, tempted to call the nurses

but she thought better of it. She cradled the phone next to her face, hoping it would ring with some news of David. Any news. Good or bad. It just had to be better than not knowing.

She tried to will herself to sleep and it didn't work. She switched to deep breathing exercises to quiet her overwrought mind and bodyv, and she fell into a light slumber. It was 1.30 am when she woke up. The neighbours' bungalow to the left was in darkness except for a dim light from their veranda. The beach was deserted. It was low tide and the surf had receded into the distance. The wide expanse of exposed seabed rippled with an eerie glimmer under the stars. A waft of cool air bearing the smell of brine and dead fish floated in through the window. Silence. Not even the mangy beach dogs were awake. She was still clutching the phone, her knuckles taut and white.

MATTEO

As expected, his drinking buddies had all left by this time of the night. Too much sun and too much beer throughout the day had enervated them. This coupled with their usual high decibel bluster about the waves they conquered and the chicks they scored made for another exhausting session at the pub, a favourite haunt for surfers and a handful of backpacking tourists as well as some locals on the make. It served a good fry up and cheap, tasty Indonesian food. And of course, the beer was always cold.

He was tired. At thirty-six, the high jinks of the younger lads of this surfing fraternity were less amusing than they used to be. Now, they were just loud and tiresome and mostly stupid. But the boys had all the energy in the world and they were a harmless distraction after a full day of surfing. Not one of them would have

known that in his other life he was one of the owners of a popular chain of restaurants back home. The challenges of starting up a business often felt insurmountable but he and his friends back home had made it work. Despite all the odds stacked against them. They were young, stubborn, perhaps even arrogant enough to think that they had all the resources and the will required to make their first venture together profitable.

They were an odd group of misfits too: the MBA grad who loved to surf more than anything else, the sound recordist who preferred to spend his weekends playing bass at the seediest grunge gigs in the city, the substance-dependent chef with the fervent dream of cooking for his own restaurant, the handsome bartender who was dying to work anywhere but behind the bar, and the IT geek who had amassed a small fortune when his partners and he decided to sell their dot com to a multinational conglomerate.

The idea for the restaurant surfaced during one of their drinking sessions at his apartment, a couple of them had also been popping an assortment of pills. The mood was amiable and light-hearted. The gathering took several meandering courses as they desultorily navigated discussions on music, clubbing, movies and food. And then the idea to pool their resources to start up a restaurant popped up. Just like that. Someone had mentioned that a space had opened up in a neighbourhood that was getting gentrified and increasingly trendy. The rental was still cheap and they even had the option to buy, which they did later.

Steady profits from their restaurants meant he could skive off work for months in a year to escape to the best surfing spots the world had to offer. From Spain, to Costa Rica, to Australia and all the way to Indonesia. He didn't feel as if he was quite

ready for Hawaii yet. But it was Bali that he kept returning to most frequently. Something about the place got under his skin. It was as if he was meant to be there year after year, if only to stay for a week. And being a solitary creature he didn't mind making this annual pilgrimage alone. No girlfriends to sully his plans for the perfect surfing experience although girls were aplenty on the beach. And when he did come close to the perfect surfing experience, it was almost like religious rapture. Or as close as he would ever get to God.

And so whenever he was surfing in the south, either in Uluwatu, Padang-Padang or Bingin, he would make his way to this drinking hole. For a quick hot meal and a drink before he retired for the night. Serious surfers like him were early risers, often up before sunrise to catch the best waves. Long before the hordes of amateurs and tourists crowded the beaches.

At almost the same time each night, the blonde girl would come into the pub. She had been coming here for three nights in a row. Always alone. She was very pretty with short-cropped blonde hair and a slight, boyish figure. She would look for the same table in the front, facing the busy street and the beach. She would never make eye contact with anyone. In her hands, as always, a book, her mobile phone and two packs of cigarettes.

Her arrival usually coincided with his departure but lately he would linger for a few minutes just to watch her nightly ritual as she settled in at her table. She would place her pink pashmina on the back of her chair, folding it over with military precision. After adjusting her chair at the exact angle she wanted, she would sit. Then she placed the book on the extreme left, the two cigarette packs side by side in the centre and her mobile phone on the outer

right. She would make sure all the items were lined up carefully with one another and then she ordered her beer. It was the same routine for the past three nights. And she did it all with a kind of rabid concentration that staved off any interruptions or unwanted attention from the mostly male patrons of the pub.

She took out one cigarette, lit it and took a long hard drag on it. She finished it quickly and started on another, finished it and went on to yet another in rapid succession. When her plastic lighter didn't work, she pushed her chair back and stood up, momentarily disoriented. She turned towards the bar where he was sitting and then doubled back for her mobile phone.

'I'm sorry. Can I borrow a lighter from someone? Or ... buy a box of matches, please,' she asked in a tired voice, barely audible.

He reached for his Zippo and gestured that he would light her cigarette. She nodded, she drew on the cigarette and then thanked him. She looked up at him, gave him a tentative smile as if she was going to say something more but she thought better of it and turned to walk back to her table.

He had always known that he was attractive, better looking than the average surfer. He was mostly inured to the attention. Most of the other girls would have gabbed on without a care. From the most outrageous come-on lines fuelled by the courage of excess alcohol or the understanding that these holiday encounters were meant to be fun, anonymous and meaningless. Over the years, he had lost count of all the girls with whom he had shared a quick romp in the most inconvenient places like the beach, under the cover of a couple of surfboards, in a vacant public toilet, or the relative privacy of so many cheap, cramped guesthouse rooms.

There had been too many nameless, faceless girls that he had

chalked up to his total surfing experience. Perhaps there were one or two somewhat meaningful encounters but none that lasted too long after the surfing season. But passing years had come with a measure of discretion for him. Those types of conquests bored him now. Much too easy. These days, his real achievement came from blending into the background with complete ease, and creating a comfortable space for his solitary sojourns.

She was smoking her cigarettes in quick succession again, lighting a new stick with the still lit stump of her old one before stubbing it out. He was about to pay for his tab and leave when her mobile phone rang with a shrill intrusion. She gave a start of surprise. But she didn't answer it. She just stared at it as if mesmerised. The ringing stopped and started again. She closed her eyes and picked it up. She looked at the caller's displayed number but made no effort to answer it.

He turned to finish his drink and asked for his bill. It was just a short walk to the popular surfers' hotel just around the corner. He was tired. All he wanted to do was to strip naked and tumble into bed. Alone. For the first time in so many years he was actually missing home, his life, his job, the routine chaos of the restaurants. Even the women whom he had been dating off and on. He missed their familiarity, their warmth. No strings attached, he had always cautioned them. He was always gentle with them. Not wanting to be the cad about town. But they knew he was not one to be rushed into any commitment. And here he was toying with the idea of actually cutting this trip short. Just to be with them.

Just as he walked past her table, the girl laid her hand on his arm. She was still seated but she had been gathering her things as

if to leave too.

'Please wait for me.'

He was expecting the usual end-of-the-night lusty proposition but she was still packing her things, not even looking at him. This one was definitely different. He shrugged and waited at the front of the pub, smoking his last cigarette for the night while he looked at the surf from across the small street. The tide was coming in, wave upon wave pounding on the sand with increased vigour. She came out and stood beside him. She was holding on to her things and the pashmina with both arms across her chest, as if to shield herself.

'Will you walk with me on the beach? Please.'

He gave her a long hard look then. She was still staring out at the surf. Around them, the wind was gaining in ferocity. She turned to him and met his gaze with luminous sapphire blue eyes.

'Nothing more,' she whispered. 'The five days are up.'

He had no idea what she meant but it was good enough for now. He led her, his hand lightly on her elbow, and they walked to the beach.

HOLIEST WHORE
IN PARADISE

Erni hadn't always been a prostitute. When she first boarded the big boneshaker of a bus that took her from her small village in the hills of East Java, she had been assured of a good job as a shampoo girl in a small salon in Sanur. And for a spell that was exactly what she did, shampooing and massaging the bored local wives of expats. These women's husbands were rich old *bule*s from Europe, North America or Australia on their second or third marriage, this time with an exotic young Indonesian who gave them a new lease on life.

The wives were well fed and well clothed in all the latest styles offered by the smart boutiques of Seminyak. They lived in beautiful spacious homes with their beautiful hybrid babies. But they were always complaining. They complained about their houses, their cars, their husbands. They complained about the lack of sex, and they complained about a surfeit of it. They complained about their husbands' parsimony: with time, with affection or with money. An endless litany spawned by petty jealousies and boredom.

Erni would go home at night to the small boarding room that she shared with three other girls from the salon, mentally

and physically exhausted from the day, her hands red and raw from the continuous shampooing and all the other hair treatment chemicals she was asked to handle. She worked in that salon for almost a year when the owners decided to sell the place. There was some kind of dispute between the partners – one of them was accused of skimming from the profits. Towards the end there were almost daily arguments right in the shop. Even though these altercations took place in the small store-room in the rear, they were audible and rancorous enough for all to hear. Gossipy clients would ask that the hairdryers be switched off for a moment so that they could eavesdrop on the backroom bickering.

And so Erni was out of job without enough money to go home. She cried herself to sleep for a week, despairing that she would be forced to start begging and sleeping on the beach or on the roadside like one of those itinerant women from Karangasem always seen carrying their babies while they pleaded for small change. Then one of the girls said that there was an opening in a café. It was a waitressing job and she was worried that she couldn't speak English but the owners assured her that all that was necessary was a pretty face, a trim figure and a friendly disposition.

She borrowed two blouses from her friend Ria, these would be worn with the sole pair of jeans in her possession. The jeans were a hand-me-down from Ayu, her cousin; they got too tight for her after the birth of her first child. Erni started work at 6.30 pm every evening; she had been advised by Ibu Artini, the owner, that she had to put on some make-up. She had never applied any cosmetics to her face. Her father was a stern Muslim who disapproved of such vanity. He said that make-up was

inconvenient and a waste of good money, especially when one should be taking their ablutions at least five times a day for prayers.

Ria taught her how to use make-up, and style her hair. She was still painfully shy and so ignorant about the ways of the world. She teetered around on the two-inch heels Ria had lent her. It soon became obvious to everyone that the men who came to the café found her naiveté and beauty a heady mix. They would ask for her as soon as they arrived, relishing her company as they drank their beer or *arak*.

For the most part they were aware of her innocence and they remained well behaved. Only once or twice did a few of them falter as they became inebriated. They stroked her on her thighs or pretended to accidentally touch her breasts. Each time she would jump in shock or shriek so loudly they would be instantly contrite. But she noticed how some of the other girls behaved with the men, teasing and taunting them with lingering touches, sliding up to them so close on the bench that they were almost on top of them, nearly in the men's laps. In turn, the men would grin happily, sitting with one arm proprietarily over the girls' shoulders, their fingertips tantalising close to the girls' pert breasts, barely covered by their corsets and sheer lace *kebaya*. For their part, these girls would be rewarded with a generous tip or little gifts.

She never knew what she was until she heard the taunts of the boys from the village nearby. It was a hot day and she had been waiting in the shade of the mango tree for Dwi when the boys appeared, gyrating their hips and making lewd signs, calling out. *'Café Cewek, Café Cewek! Cewek Café, Cewek Café!'* What they said wasn't rude in itself but their expressions and gestures left no

doubt as to the intended slur. Then one of their mothers appeared, and shouted at them to behave, and the boys stopped, but not before they gave one last defiant chorus of jeers before they fled, leaving echoes of raucous laughter and clouds of dust as they ran to the rice fields to continue their spirited horse-play.

She noticed that the women of the village weren't exactly affable with any of the workers from the café, in particular the girls. The women were never rude, always offering merely the barest amount of courtesies but there was never any friendly interest or sociable banter. And none of the men from the village dared to walk into the café, only those from farther afield, those men who felt confident enough to be there without question, protected by a certain degree of anonymity.

So she was now a 'café girl' and by the way the café clientele behaved and the manner in which the villagers were aloof, she knew she was just a few degrees better than a prostitute. She had become the type of woman surely to be shunned in her village; a woman who brought shame and ignominy to her community. But it was just a job to her and she knew that she wasn't doing anything that was obviously wrong according to the teachings of her religion. She still considered herself among the faithful despite the free flow of alcohol at the café. After all, she imbibed none herself, and she observed the five prayer times that were the cornerstone of her faith.

But things changed soon after. Dwi, her best friend, got involved with a wealthy married man from Jembrana. He offered her his hand in marriage as his second wife. Dwi wasn't sure at first because she would have to give up her faith and become a Hindu but the man seemed genuinely enamoured with her. Plus

the material perks of such a union were irresistible, especially when it meant that her family back in Java could live in comfort on all the money she could now send home to them every month. So her one friend and protector had been whisked off to live in a pretty little bungalow in a housing estate where the middle-class locals lived. As far as Dwi's neighbours were concerned she was his only wife and they were a happily married couple beginning a new life together.

Erni missed Dwi very much at the *kos*. Her easy laughter, her generosity and her street-smart advice on life, especially on men, made it all bearable. She didn't feel homesick when Dwi had been around. The other girls were too self-absorbed or too engrossed in their competition to ensnare a better catch than Dwi's.

It was around then that Komang appeared. He was younger than most of the other clients and he could speak very good English. The first time he walked into the café he came with a burly, sandy-haired middle-aged Englishman, Paul, who seemed to sweat profusely from every pore of his skin. The *bule*'s colourful Hawaiian shirt was drenched around his neck, underarms and back. His crimson skin beamed bright – it seemed to compete for attention with the florid shirt. He was generous with his money, buying a round of drinks for everyone, lavishing his attention on the girls like an incestuous older uncle. For his efforts, the girls fought with one another to be his favourite one. He became a regular after that and Komang would wait patiently in the corner until Paul was successful enough to persuade one of the girls to go back with him for the night.

Because of his rather worldly and aloof manner (and of course, his rather good looks), the girls tried to get Komang's attention

too. This was despite the knowledge that the other patrons were probably better providers than he. But he seemed oblivious of their attention; instead he would speak at length only to Ibu Artini or the other male employers at the café. But throughout the night his eyes would drift back to Erni. Her soft-spoken ways and gentle demeanour seemed to intrigue him more and more each time he set his eyes on her. At first he thought it was all an act on her part: a ruse to reel in the men foolish enough to fall for it or a ploy to part them from their money. But she never faltered. He could tell that she was genuinely aggrieved each time any of the men misbehaved with her. Her skin would be flushed red with shame and anger and she would be very quiet. He knew it wasn't exactly the behaviour of a seasoned pro.

Komang knew just the way he would approach and befriend Erni. He had studied her carefully and he felt that he had come to understand her character. He knew he had to be respectful and polite. He would never make the mistake of flirting with any of the other girls or even being mildly inebriated in front of her. Instead he would gain her confidence by being nothing like any of the other men who came in here. His perfect opportunity came one night when a particularly difficult customer started to manhandle her; when she rebuffed the drunk's attentions he became abusive. Komang who was used to handling the most belligerent drunks in Kuta – drunks who came from every corner of the known world – stepped in lithely. First Komang spoke gently but firmly and when that provoked the man into taking a wild swing at him, Komang deftly put him in a choke-hold and the man was immobilised, gagging and spluttering as he fell to the floor on his knees.

Erni came to talk to him after that incident. She shyly

thanked him and he offered to send her home but she demurred. But Komang insisted and she felt obliged after his rescue. The lifts home became a regular arrangement each time Komang appeared at the café. Sometimes he would take her for a quick drink at one of the small *warung*s, a hot tea or a quiet drive before sending her back to her *kos*. Komang knew better than to touch her but one day while they were driving on the deserted streets of Denpasar, he reached out for her hand. She didn't flinch and so he drove all the way back with one hand on the steering wheel and the other clasping hers.

Erni would always remember that first moment when Komang reached out and touched her hand. It felt like the most natural thing but her heart was beating so hard that she could feel the pounding in her head. A week after that he kissed her. It was her very first kiss. They were driving on a dark, quiet street and he pulled over suddenly. He reached out and pulled her close to him and kissed her forcefully on her lips. She was surprised but the pleasure left her too weak to stop him. Her remaining sense of decorum disappeared altogether soon after and she let him pull her even closer to him, his tongue deep in her mouth, then moving to her ears and neck. She wasn't quite sure what to do so she mirrored each move he made. She remembered how Komang seemed to like it when she did that.

She felt powerless to refuse Komang anything he asked of her. He was the only source of stability and affection in her life especially with her best friend Dwi now gone. To his credit, Komang treated her with gentleness and concern that she had never felt with any man before. In her mind, he was the one – the man whom would rescue her from the café, the man with whom

she would spend the rest of her life. She was willing to change her religion when they got married, so that their children would be of the same faith as their father's. She had carefully planned all the details of their future together.

She knew that her instincts about him were right when he told her that he wanted to bring her home to Tabanan to meet his parents. That night in the back seat of his car, as they were passionately kissing each other, both half undressed, she let him enter her. 'Are you sure?' he had asked her softly and she nodded. When he had entered her, she cried quietly into his shoulder, biting down on her bottom lip until it bled.

* * *

She never thought about sin after that. She had ceased to hear her father's voice, his endless sermons on how to be a better Muslim. She had always fallen short of his expectations in his eyes. That was one of the reasons she had made the decision to leave the family house. When her mother died, she was expected to cook and clean and look after her three younger siblings and her father. He was a man who hardly spoke to his children except to chide them or to preach about some Islamic tenet that they had failed to grasp. There was never any affection from him: no hugs nor tender words of encouragement or love.

And yet she still felt the compulsion to pray until today. This was her mother's legacy. Her mother had taught them the practice of the faith. She gave Quran reading lessons to all the children in the village. Her mother was a much-loved woman. She never uttered a harsh word to anyone or about anyone. She

was perpetually smiling and always affectionate with the children, even the ones who would rather cut class to play in the fruit orchards. When her mother died, the whole village mourned. After that, her father became more withdrawn and sterner. All the children tiptoed around the house, whispering to one another lest their father heard any of their conversation. They were sure to be reprimanded, or worse still punished, for falling short of his exacting standards.

With Komang, sin and hell-fire were farthest from her mind. She felt loved and she returned that love without reservations. Having sex with him was a natural part of that equation. But she became pregnant and that changed everything. Komang was supportive but he wasn't ready for a baby. He said that he still needed to save more money from his job as a tour guide before they could get house and start a family. While the sin of fornication was something she could live with, aborting a baby was mortifying to her. It was murder and everything she had been taught made her certain that it was truly her one-way ticket to hell. But Komang was adamant. He said they would only be ready to start a family in about two years' time.

She hoped and prayed that he would change his mind. But right till the last moment at the clinic all he did was try to reassure her that everything would be all right once they were through with the procedure. She was silent. 'Please God forgive me, God forgive me, God forgive me …' was the phrase that kept going through her mind during the trip to the dingy little clinic and even as the nurses made her spread her legs and put her feet through the stirrups. She remembered how they thrust the cold hard steel of the speculum into her and they tried to prise the instrument

open but it wouldn't budge. The nurse said, 'The smaller one' and she just tried to shut out the pain, all sensations, all sounds and all her emotions during the D&C. She kept reciting in her head all the verses of the Quran that she could remember and she kept her eyes focused on the ceiling.

She left the clinic pallid and unsteady on her feet. She just couldn't bring herself to utter a single word to the doctor or the nurses, or even to Komang. He brought her back to his boarding room after that. She couldn't bear to look at him straight in the eyes. She lay down on her side on his single bed, facing the wall with her back towards him. He was extremely gentle with her, feeding her porridge and washing her with a small towel as if she were a baby. She just kept her eyes on the wall, reciting all the Quranic verses she could remember to assuage her guilt.

Komang reached out for her during the night from his makeshift bed on the floor just to make sure she was okay but she just couldn't bring herself to touch him. When she was sure he was fast asleep, she made her way to the bathroom. She saw how her dark blood had soaked through her underwear right onto her sarong and with her fist in her mouth so that Komang would not hear, she wept some more in the bathroom. She washed the panties and the sarong carefully and returned to the room. And in the dead of night as Komang and all the neighbours slept peacefully, she went behind his *kos,* to the small backyard and burnt the underwear and sarong there.

The bleeding didn't stop as it was supposed to. There was a complication and Komang had to bring her to the clinic again. She had to undergo another surgical procedure and then the doctor told them that she could never have a baby. She looked at the

doctor in disbelief. Komang was silent, he was lost in his thoughts and too remorseful to give voice to any of them. He reached out to squeeze her hand but his was ice-cold. She knew their relationship had ended at that very moment. She felt worthless as a woman. As a prospective wife to Komang, or to any other man, she had nothing to offer. She had always wanted to have children, to start a new life in Bali with a family of her own. But this was her punishment. She walked out on him a few nights soon after that. He was fast asleep on the floor, snoring gently with one arm over his eyes. She gently stroked his arm, gathered all her things and she left him sleeping peacefully on the floor.

With all the money she had saved she bought a cheap air ticket to Jakarta and she found herself a new job. She started as a waitress in a small restaurant but a friend said that she could earn almost thrice her salary if she didn't mind the late hours of working at a small karaoke lounge. She was told that all she had to do was to encourage the men to drink the more expensive spirits from the bar, and she had the freedom to decide just how far she was willing to go if the men started to get frisky. For Erni it sounded a lot like her old job at the café except this time her clientele were city slickers with a lot more money and less gentility. Sexual assignations after hours were discussed openly and all the girls were blasé about them.

Despite the handsome gifts they offered, she just couldn't bring herself to leave with any of the men at the end of the night, even if it was merely for a cup of coffee. In the lounge, she entertained them and put up with their endless propositions and cajoling, she even learnt how to tolerate some of their drunken groping without retaliating with an outright slap. But she made it

clear that she was not about to let them kiss her or touch her like they did with the other girls. Sex was definitely out of the picture. She went home alone each night in the old, beaten-up taxi driven by a kindly old man, Pak Sudarso who kept a watchful eye on her. Each time there would be a warm packet of *bakso* or *nasi goreng* waiting for her in the cab, a late night supper she would eat when she got to her boarding room.

The one night that Pak Sudarso took ill, her life was catapulted onto another direction. The catalyst was Djoko, a rich young man who frequented the lounge with a group of boisterous big-spenders. She was standing on the curb, waiting for a taxi when he slowed down in his red BMW. He wound down his window and offered her a lift home even though her working-class neighbourhood was miles out of the way to his well-manicured upper-class home. He had his own condo but he preferred the comfort and convenience of his parent's six-bedroom mansion with its retinue of servants and gardeners, if he was not entertaining a young woman or not too drunk to risk the censure of his father, a former military man.

Djoko was always attentive to her but he knew that with a lot less effort he could bed any of the other girls at the lounge. After all, beautiful girls were not a rare commodity at the lounge or anywhere else in Jakarta. But Erni was definitely an enigma. She had dignity and poise uncommon for a lounge worker and this made her particularly enticing. And of course her refusal to sleep with any of the patrons made her even more of a challenge for them. In jest they would place bets with one another to see who would be man enough to 'break the ice' with Erni. But when all failed, the wager became a standing joke amongst the regulars.

Erni was under no illusions about Djoko. She had seen his

drunken frolicking too often not to understand what the young man was all about. That he had money and good looks made him even more reckless and cavalier with the girls. She was not happy about jumping into a car with such a man. But that night the new shoes she wore had given her blisters and she was tired. At about eight in the evening Ibu Wati, Pak Sudarso's wife, had called to say that her husband was too ill to drive the cab that night and asked if Erni could find her own way home. It was after 2 am and there were no taxis, *ojek*s or *bemo*s to be had in that part of the city. It was eerily silent as if the city was under an emergency curfew.

'I won't hurt you. What kind of monster do you think I am? I'm just trying to help you. *Kasian deh* …' Djoko kept repeating this again and again as she refused his offer of a lift home. She kept looking back at the club, hoping someone would come through the doors and rescue her. But the only ones to come out were Susi and her regular customer Pak Tjipto who was so drunk that Susi had to support him as he stumbled along the pavement to his waiting car and chauffeur. Erni walked toward them hurriedly, she knew she was better off getting a lift with them than with Djoko but he leapt out of the car and waved them off, gesturing that Erni would ride with him.

She didn't have much choice after that. And the prospect of sleeping in the club was just too distasteful to her. She had a good idea what some of the girls did with the men in the private rooms. They would often boast about their escapades, showing off the trinkets that they received from these men for all their extra services. Most of the men were old enough to be their fathers and this was the fact that was the source of greatest dismay to Erni.

That greed and lust always seemed to override any remaining sense of human decency.

She uttered a quick '*Bismillah*' and she stepped into his car. Djoko was grinning widely, he turned up the volume on his car stereo before he swerved onto the road and sped away. He kept sipping from a small metal flask the entire time he was driving. He shoved the flask into her face, and asked her to take a swig but she refused. He kept insisting and she kept saying no. He became quiet and withdrawn after that, his earlier buoyant mood completely gone. And then all of a sudden he stopped the car in a quiet, unlit parking lot in front of a row of shophouses.

'Do you think I don't know you're just playing a game? Do you think we're all so stupid that we don't know you're just a common whore? You're no virgin,' Djoko hissed at her, pinning her down with one arm holding the car door on her side.

'Just send me home, Mas. You promised you would. Please.'

'Are you a virgin? Answer me first,' he demanded but Erni just kept silent and he became more incensed. He thrust his hand into her lap and starting digging between her legs. 'Show me.' He kept saying 'Show me' as he exerted more force, moving his body on top of hers.

She was crying and pleading but he was like a man possessed. His hand was under her skirt now, roughly finding its way to her panties, and tearing it off. She screamed and screamed until her vocal chords could make no more sound. 'Show me what you have.'

He forced a finger, two and his whole hand into her. The pain was excruciating. Her whole body shook with each sob. His other hand was around her throat now, a vice-like grip. 'Shush …

Keep quiet. Enjoy this.' She went limp, a combination of fear and exhaustion.

'Come on, co-operate. You have to move a little.' He kissed her on her mouth, pushing his tongue deep into her mouth until she gagged. He grabbed her breasts roughly, tore open her shirt and then he started sucking on her like a hungry baby. This seemed to excite him more and he unzipped himself and penetrated her forcefully. She tried to scream again but couldn't. Tears kept streaming down her face, her neck, her chest. Her tears wet his face, his shirt as he pressed down on her.

He stopped after a few minutes. He was spent. He seemed contrite then, as if suddenly aware of what he had done. He asked Erni for forgiveness. But she just kept on crying soundlessly. Djoko stepped out of the car, had a cigarette and, in silence, he sent her straight home.

* * *

Erni didn't return to the lounge after that night. Her boss called her several times over the week but she said that she was too ill to work. About three days after the incident, a man came to her *kos* and delivered a sealed brown envelope. It was from Djoko. There was 5 million rupiah in it. There was no note from him. She used the money to leave Jakarta. She went back to her village but not much had changed there. Her family was happy to see her but her father was still as cold and distant as ever, his religious pronouncements were now more severe with the passing years. She stayed there for two weeks and then she made a decision to return to Bali. It had been three years since she had left the island.

She found her way back to Sanur. Her decision to become a prostitute was based purely on monetary considerations. She tried working at an Italian *trattoria* for about a month but the wage was too low and the tips were not enough for her to support her family back in Java. Djoko had taken away the last vestiges of her self-respect. By keeping his money she felt that she was no better than a prostitute.

* * *

The first time she had sex for money in Sanur she felt numb. The voices in her head were dead. There was no right or wrong. She kept telling herself that her body was just a shell. The man was a tourist, a lonely middle-aged traveller who came to Bali frequently. Kurt was soft-spoken and clean. He advised her to demand that all her sexual partners wore condoms. He paid for the entire night and she followed him to his hotel on the beach. They talked for most of the night. He asked her questions about herself and he told her about his life back in Europe. She didn't understand most of what he said but she was grateful for his gentle ways. He took off her dress and he held her in his arms tenderly before they had sex.

She spent many more nights with Kurt. When he left Bali, she felt bereft. He was not merely a customer to whom she plied her body. He had become a friend and confidante, the first in a long time. But he had given her enough money so that she could bide her time until her next customer. She learnt to read the men who frequented the nightspots around Sanur. There were some whom appeared very placid but once they had too much alcohol they

were abusive. There were some who requested despicable acts and she vowed she would never be with such men no matter how much they offered. She learnt to pick lonely men who wanted companionship more than sex; men she could be with for more than one night. That way what she did seemed less like prostitution and more like a contractual relationship. But she made a firm rule never to take any local men as her customer. Her experience with Komang and Djoko sealed her resolve.

With the passing years, she received many marriage proposals from the tourists and expatriates she met but she was determined to make and save more money for her family and for herself. She was frugal with the money she earned. She didn't spend it on clothes or make-up like the other girls. She invested in English classes and she bought books on self-improvement. More than anything she wanted a new life that didn't depend on her being on her back night after night, subject to a man's moods or sexual whims. She wanted independence, a small house of her own so that she could bring her sisters and brothers from Java to live with her. They could learn new skills here, start a small business together.

She went home to her village at least once a year for Eid. She had stopped fasting in Ramadhan for many years, in her mind she could not reconcile what she did for a living and maintaining the practice of her faith. But she gave alms. Every year, right before Eid, she rode her motorbike all the way to Gianyar to donate money and rice to a Muslim orphanage. There were 300 children crammed in the small facility, unwanted children who had lost their parents to death, divorce or some other reversal in fortune. Her child with Komang, if it had been allowed to live, could have

easily ended up in that place.

Through the years she had managed to get by without a pimp but some of the girls weren't so lucky. Some of the pimps were husbands or boyfriends who had no qualms about living off the drudgery and misery of these women. Many of the girls thought that it would be an easy way out of a life of poverty and hunger. But most of them were realistic and stoic about their prospects. For many, the only solace was looking ahead to a better future with a foreign husband who would rescue them, take them away to Europe or North America or Australia where they could stay in a condo or a small, pretty house in a suburb. Failing that, they were perfectly happy to belong to the community of local women who were married to the older *bules*, living in a beautiful bungalow with a nice garden in Sanur, Ubud, Canggu or Umalas. Their children could grow up proud and beautiful. There was security in that kind of future.

Some of the younger girls looked up to Erni. They respected her because she was wise and kind. She was always ready to offer money or assistance when any of the girls got into any trouble. Like an older sister, she doled out advice and commiseration for anyone who came to her door. Some of them ended up sleeping on her floor for weeks while trying to figure out what to do and where to go next. Erni had given a few of them money for their bus fare home, back to villages up north, on the east coast or somewhere in Java. Some of the girls started to ask her to manage their work; they wanted to save money for their family back home and a few of them needed a nest egg so that they could quit prostitution and begin a new life after a few years.

Erni had a natural aptitude for such tasks. At first she managed

these girls' money for free but after more and more asked her for help she began to charge a nominal fee. The girls were quite happy to give her any sum she requested because they were certain of her honesty and diligence. Erni still had a few regular customers but managing the girls took up most of her time. She was now able to rent a small house in Sanur. She had a maid, Laksmi, one of the younger girls who couldn't stomach prostitution after trying it out for a few weeks.

* * *

At thirty-five, Erni was still a desirable woman. She was confident of her skills managing the girls under her and of her own talents as a prostitute. She had learnt to master enough sexual techniques and social graces to keep the men coming back for more. Her regular clients were expatriates who resided permanently on the island. There were a few who made annual trips to Bali for business mixed with pleasure. It wasn't a bad life. In the small community of women like her, she was sought after and respected. In the past year, she had been investing in property on the advice of one of her favourite regulars, Raymond. She bought small plots of land just outside prime areas, which were bought up by the villa developers and other foreigners wanting to have a share in this version of paradise. Already she had sold off three pieces of land to one of these developers for a handsome profit.

Everything seemed to be right on course until her father died. His heart gave up early one morning while he was sweeping the yard of their house in East Java. When one of her brothers found him, the ducks and the chickens were clustered around him,

pecking him as if he were a big sack of feed. Her brothers dragged him unceremoniously into the kitchen, not quite sure what they should do with him. They sat looking at his corpse for at least three hours before they decided to call for help from some of the other villagers. They rang Erni in the evening, their voices hushed and apologetic as if scared they would still provoke their father's displeasure with the noise.

She left for her village as soon as she had packed a small bag and found someone willing to drive her all the way home. When she arrived the small house was all lit, it was filled with villagers reciting the *Yasin* for the all-night vigil. Her father would not have been happy with the gathering. She could almost hear his voice berating her for not burying him earlier. After all it was the prescribed thing to do; Muslim dead should be buried as soon as possible. There should not be any displays of sorrow. When she entered the house, her siblings were huddled in a corner, too bewildered and too tired to do anything but hold each other and look at their guests in silence.

When she saw them she broke down. She cried and cried, inconsolable by her siblings' hugs or her aunts' gentle soothing words. She cried for her brothers and sisters and she cried for her mother and the fact she still missed her despite all the years since her death. She cried for her father and she cried for her relief that he was now dead. She cried for all the years that she had spent wishing for his death so that she and her brothers and sisters could be freed from his subtle tyranny. She cried for her life and her lost innocence.

She couldn't remember falling asleep that night but she did. She dreamt her mother had come back for the funeral; she looked

serene and as always in the past, full of love and affection for everyone. The family clung to her, not wanting to let her go. Her mother said that there was still so much for Erni to do. That her brothers and sisters needed her more than ever now. That it would be a time of change for everyone. She cried when her mother said she had to go back, the pain was as real as the time when she died, leaving them to fend for themselves. Erni woke up sobbing, tears streaming down her cheeks.

* * *

She stayed in Java for two weeks and then she returned to her home in Sanur. Some of the girls were frantic in her absence. One had a problem with a stalker, another had a drug addict ex-boyfriend who was trying to extort money from her. Then there were the others who needed to make withdrawals from their accounts for miscellaneous reasons: from wanting to buy a new dress to having to pay for a child's school fees. She handled all their concerns calmly and efficiently but inside she was wracked with agonising guilt. What if her mother could see her now? Handling all these ill-gotten gains? *Uang haram.* And what would her mother say if she started seeing her own customers again? What would her mother say if she could see Erni allowing the men to do all that they did to her in bed? There would be no peace for her mother in the afterlife. Erni's life went against everything her mother had believed in.

She maintained a confident façade with the girls but every night since her father's funeral, she cried herself to sleep. Her mother figured prominently in her thoughts, intruding on her

actions during her waking hours. Her only solace came from the moments she sat on her prayer mat. She didn't do anything at first, she just stared ahead in silence, letting all the doubt and confusion float pass her. It became her daily oasis. A moment of peace from the chaos and turmoil of her life and the demands of her girls. During one of her sessions, she decided never again to have sex with a man for money. It came to her like a revelation, a sudden thought alighting on her just as she was about to get up and fold away the mat.

She tried praying again the following day. But she kept forgetting verses and she kept forgetting the proper order of the compulsory prayer. That very same day she went to Sulawesi Road where the Muslim tradesmen in Bali had shops selling clothes, books and other paraphernalia for the faithful. She bought one of those instruction books meant for children just starting to learn their prayers. There were cartoon pictures detailing every step of the obligatory prayer and every verse that was to be recited.

And so she started praying again. One prayer a day at first, concealing this even from her maid, Laksmi, for fear the other girls would start talking about her. She administered advice to the girls about finances and sex and life with her usual quiet composure but the fissures were beginning to show. The girls had begun to notice her unexplained absences and long silences. They thought she had a secret lover. Some of her regulars were infuriated with her refusal to have sex with them despite her offer to get younger and prettier girls as her replacement. The only person who didn't question her was Raymond. When she told him that she could no longer have sex with him, all he said was that he would wait for her until she was ready again.

She felt as if she would never be ready again. She had found some peace of mind in spite of the double life she was leading. She had brought over her youngest sister and two of her brothers to live with her. The two older ones chose to remain in the family house in Java. She told her family that she was running an employment agency and that was why the girls needed frequent consultation with her.

She now kept up all her obligatory prayers, facing Mecca five times a day as she sought forgiveness from God and her mother. Those were the only moments of tranquillity that she had amidst her doubt and confusion. It allowed her to feel close to her mother again. She knew that there was still much she had to do to atone for all her transgressions but she couldn't find the courage to sever all ties. And how would she earn enough money to support her family and help out the girls who needed her? The girls and the men who sought them were her life. No ready answers came to her and so she prayed and prayed for some direction.

* * *

One evening, Raymond appeared at her house. A furtive knock on the door and there he was, looking sheepish and uncomfortable. Her sister and her brothers were just clearing up the table after dinner. It was Laksmi's night off. She was surprised to see him there without a word of notice. It was unlike him. Their dates had always been at his house. He would sometimes send her home in the morning but he was never invited into her house. He proposed to her, right on the doorstep, bearing a small diamond ring in his hand. She was speechless, totally taken aback by the ring and his

earnestness. She didn't say no but she couldn't agree to marriage when her life was in such a state of flux. She told him she needed more time to think. He said that he was willing to wait, no matter how long it would take.

She didn't sleep that night. She prayed the entire night, trying to obtain divine guidance for what she should do next. It was almost dawn and she was beginning to feel drowsy. She was still sitting on her prayer mat, one hand grasping her prayer beads. Outside, the roosters were crowing away and her Balinese neighbours were already stirring in their family compounds, readying themselves for their morning chores.

Her future was filled with questions. The road ahead was so clear one moment and then just as quickly the clarity disappeared, overrun by fear and doubt. Like a mirage on a sun-scorched day. But she had more options now. All the choices she had made in the past had been thrust upon her. Out of sheer desperation mostly. And she was alone then. Now her family were with her. They needed her. Her extended family of Laksmi and the girls still needed her. Raymond needed a wife – and he was waiting for her.

She got up and folded her prayer mat. She bathed and put on one of her mother's old *kebaya*s and a sarong. She took out a long scarf and wore it around her head. Like a good Muslim woman. Maybe if she looked the part, she might start believing it herself. People might start believing it. There was still so much work for her to do. So many people depended on her and she couldn't fail them. Perhaps the best choice was not to choose. Not yet, not now.

THE LADY OF THE VILLA

Caroline watched the rain pour down on her lotus buds. The heavy sheets of water pummelled the blossoms until they were bent, almost touching the surface of the pond. They were done for. Rivulets were flowing all around her beautiful garden and there was a small pool forming on the veranda. She could see the puddle growing by the minute, the edges now touching her brand new rattan lounge chairs. Perhaps she should have opted for the synthetic wicker set after all. Those would have been more expensive but she would have been spared this bother with rain. The water was steadily pooling at the feet of the settee. She had no idea where the silly girl was. It must have been at least ten minutes since she had told the girl to mop up the puddle and bring in the furniture. The girl was so unfathomably slow.

She sighed in frustration. She looked at the three steps leading down to the garden. On each corner of the steps were hibiscus and frangipani flowers. She liked it that way, flowers artfully and meticulously laid out on the stairs, along the pebbled pathway in the garden, on the steps leading to her garage. Even her stone-carved Buddhas in the garden had them, making them look less austere, almost defiantly festive. The flowers were not quite the traditional offerings, these were more like artistic markers for her daily movements in her new home. She had painstakingly designed each mini bouquet of blossoms and taught her maid how

to arrange them. Of course the girl was good with her hands. All the Balinese were. Especially the women who had to do their offerings day after day. But her lovely creations were so forlorn-looking now. Drenched. As if someone had soaked them in a pail for an hour. And there was still no sign of that girl.

'Putu,' she bellowed, once into the garden, more out of extreme annoyance than anything else. Then she turned around and shouted the name again in the direction of the kitchen. But there was still no sign of the girl. Deaf. And daft. The girl had forced her to yell out loud, like a peasant. It was just undignified; no way for a lady of the house to behave. No way at all.

Caroline knew it would have been a lot better if she had a houseboy. A docile, quietly capable young man who could act as her valet-cum-driver. There would certainly be none of this girlish petulance. The constant tardiness. As if each simple task required superhuman feats. One would think Putu was conscripted to build the pyramids the way she was always so lethargic and sullen. Indeed she would not have picked this girl had she been given the choice. But she had none. The girl came with the house. A fait accompli. 'You want to rent the house? Well, it comes with the girl too.' The owner's wife's cousin's niece.

But she knew she had to let a few more months go by before putting her foot down. Think of some diplomatic excuse to release her from employment; she would have to pick her words very carefully so as not to let anyone lose face. This was what her friend Tess advised. Tess, the Bali veteran of fifteen years, was the reason Caroline had moved here. Tess could speak the language (it helped of course that her husband was Balinese) and she knew how to get her way without rocking the boat. The paramount

thing was to maintain harmony, Tess exhorted. Tess regularly resorted to convoluted explanations and circuitous methods just to achieve her objective. Make it look like a win-win situation and always lay on that extra dose of humility. That always seemed to work, Tess said.

At first, it was an untenable situation for Caroline. She had always taken pride in being forthright. Her candour was a virtue not a vice. And here she was expected to grit her teeth and pretend. Pretend to be pleased when she was irked to the brink of being incensed. Pretend to be agreeable and placid when all she wanted to do was search and destroy. Untenable, indeed. But she was slowly learning. Tess was on call to give her personal coaching on almost a daily basis. After all there was no going back. She had sold her house, her car, all her worldly possessions. They were all gone, save the most treasured. This was to be her home now. It had been her dream for years. She had to make it work.

* * *

She had searched all around Ubud for a suitable house. It took her three long months to find this house. A villa as they called it here. It was serendipitous. She had been looking for something reasonably large. A studio for her to design her jewellery and paint her landscapes. At least two bedrooms; one to accommodate guests. As it turned out, there was an assortment of free-loading visitors from home, gleefully taking advantage of her new Bali residency. But she didn't mind. The company no matter how irritating at times helped her ground herself. It made her home feel more permanent when her former life intersected with this

new one. It dispelled that odd sense of dislocation that she sometimes felt.

She had almost given up when she decided to take a drive with Wayan one Saturday afternoon. It was mainly to let off steam. To forget about houses or rental rates or purchase prices. She had grown terribly weary of the house hunt. But she was getting most weary of living out of her three suitcases. Her other belongings were still on the way by sea in a container. The vagabond existence disagreed with her disposition. She was getting increasingly tetchy with each passing day. She was beginning to find things to hate about her hotel and even the unerringly polite staff, about the town and its people.

And then one day, she saw it. Beyond the rice fields, peeking through the thick shrubbery and heavy boscage of the trees. It was tucked away just off Jalan Suweta. Accessible only through a small dirt lane. The lane was bordered on one side by the rice fields, and by a high wall of a bungalow or gallery of some sort on the other. She knew this discovery was destined. She almost jumped out of the car before it came to a complete stop, and she didn't even bother to wait for Wayan to accompany her – she just marched purposefully toward the house, swinging her wide-brimmed hat in her hand.

The property had a general air of neglect. The house itself looked rather dilapidated. But it was actually the garden or what vaguely resembled a garden that seemed the worst off. The bushes and hedges were overgrown. The flowerbeds were either a riotous mess or barren patches, burial mounds for plants once upon a time much loved but since deserted to die. The grass desperately needed mowing – it was almost thigh level, probably concealing

colonies of snakes and rodents vying for supremacy. The pond was a receptacle of malodorous stagnant water, profuse weeds and mosquito larvae. But it wasn't beyond salvation. And she was just the single-minded person to do it.

The house was a three-storey structure, the first two were split level, on a gentle slope, following the natural contours of the ravine. There was a stream flowing at the bottom of the ravine, quite difficult to get to it because of the dense undergrowth. There seemed to be a hint of some heavy stone steps leading down to the stream but these disappeared, having lost their battle with the lush vegetation. But the house was breathtaking despite its dereliction; it had wide verandas, French doors all around with wooden shutters. The top floors had wide balconies, with enough space for a day bed and a small set of table and chairs. There was judicious use of local-style wood carving and ornamentation so the house retained a solid European sensibility.

It took her three days to track down the owner of the house and within two weeks all the papers were signed. And the house was hers. Her very own villa in Bali.

So Putu came with the house and her uncle, Komang, offered himself as the gardener. Then Wayan, who was already in part-time employment, became her full-time driver. Who would have thought that she would finally be able to live her dream of owning this fine villa with an entourage of servants to assist her in running it? In no time, she had her long 'to do' list in hand and a firm determination to complete all the tasks on it, come what may.

A lot of work was required to get the villa up to her standards. So the first three months were particularly gruelling. She felt like a

drill sergeant at times, trying to motivate her staff and the gaggle of itinerant workers hired for the renovation and repairs. For the most part they were hard-working but they just weren't as rigorous and detail-oriented as she would have liked them to be. Of course language was an obstacle. It was difficult to translate her grand vision into reality when the simplest words could be misunderstood. But Tess was by her side from time to time, to interpret to the troops for her and offer succour when she got frustrated or fatigued.

But slowly and surely the improvements were made and the ramshackle house was gradually transformed into the home she had envisaged. An abode fit for her to reside in. The plaque with the villa's name came up on the outer wall the first night she slept there. Casa Bella Carolina. The silver letters had a black outline, set against a polished copper background with a filigreed bronze border. It was big enough for all to see, right on Jalan Suweta, with an arrow pointing to the back of the lane.

Some of her precious collectibles, furniture and Persian rugs arrived not long after. She took the topmost floor as her bedroom, the second floor which opened to the main entrance of the villa, had been divided into her living and dining area. Her studio and the guest bedroom were located at the lowest level. It was rather dark and damp there because of its proximity to the ravine and the stream but she liked the privacy the space afforded. And anyhow she was more likely to paint up in the dining area where the light was better. Her jewellery designing was more a hobby than an income-making venture at this point. She had spent six months in Florence learning the craft from some of the best Italian experts. Having some money allowed her the indulgence of

choice. Thankfully, her late husband had made sure that she was well taken care of when he died.

* * *

She was putting on her Italian silk caftan when she heard the dinner gong downstairs. She looked at her watch. Yes, 7.30 pm right on the dot, she smiled. Putu was getting better in some ways. She remembered how the girl sulked when she was told she had to beat the gong for dinner. It was as if Putu thought it was beneath her to do such a thing. The bronze gong was a relatively new addition to the household routine. It was her recent discovery whilst shopping for antiques in the Campuhan area. They said it had come from a *kraton* in Solo. The asking price was exorbitant but she had haggled and haggled – the shop girls had to call the owner of the shop twice at his home to get approval for the discount – and finally she intimidated them all into submission. She truly was a consummate shopper.

She took out her prized pearls from the small safe tucked away at the bottom of her armoire and she slipped it over her head. She took one long, critical look at herself in her full-length mirror and she put on her gold lamé slippers. *Sandal* they called it here and she remembered how she tried to explain to them that the terminology was wrong. They were so many things that were all topsy-turvy here but she knew they were some things that she could change, while others would just be an exercise in futility. She gave herself a few quick sprays from the crystal atomiser and she was ready.

She arrived downstairs in a cloud of purple silk and Chanel

No. 5. Putu was standing by the big custom-made teak dining table. The candles were all ceremoniously lit around its wide expanse and also on the sideboard, beneath a huge mirror which reflected the flickering golden radiance into the room. She was having baked fish with cream sauce, one of the few dishes that Putu could manage on her own without disastrous results. Caroline gave her a nod and a small smile of approval as she sat down. There was a glass of aperitif waiting beside her plate. As if on cue, Putu switched on the CD player and some soothing classical music began (was it Beethoven or Strauss, she never knew which was which) and she felt the stresses of the day lift away with a few more sips of her drink.

She smiled when she thought of the time she had invited Tess over for dinner. Poor, poor Tess, looking rather harassed, arrived at 7 pm instead of 6.30 as they had agreed. She was apologetic about being late but it was perfunctory, as if such delays were quite commonplace and to be expected. And the state she was in. She was still wearing the frock that she had been running around in since the morning. A shapeless faded cotton shift more suited to gardening than anything else. And when she saw Caroline's teal-blue shantung silk suit complemented by an exquisite lapis lazuli necklace, her jaw dropped.

'Caroline, I must say, there was no need for you to dress on my account.'

'Dress? On your account? Oh! No ... This is my usual attire for dinner.'

'You look like you're ready to dine with the Queen, my dear.'

'Look Tess ... it's quite simple. Just because I choose to live in the midst of the rice fields doesn't mean I have to dress like a

farmer. I need to hold on to some cherished traditions.'

'Traditions, Caroline? You never used to dress like this back home! And I know this for a fact. I've had dinner at your house countless times ...'

For the life of her, she just couldn't understand why Tess was so affronted by her fine clothing. And there she was coming to dinner looking like something the cat had dragged in. It was obvious that this place had got to Tess. She used to be bothered about fashion and style back in her day. And now she was vehemently casual and antagonistic to anyone else who would chose to care about their appearance. It was strange indeed. Caroline hoped that she wouldn't turn into an unkempt bohemian after a year in this town.

Well, so far, she was still able to maintain her habit of dressing for dinner, even when she was alone. Doing it kept her sane, despite what Tess and the other long-tenured expatriates might have to say about it. It really wasn't anyone's business what she did in own her villa anyway. This was her domain and everyone who came here would just have to abide by her rules. She settled back into her chair, making herself more comfortable as she sipped her glass of Chardonnay. Her dinner was quite good. She rang the silver bell on the table. Nothing. After more vigorous ringing, Putu peered from the kitchen entrance, '*Ya, Ibu?*'

She asked the girl to clear the table and requested for a new bottle of wine to be brought to the living room. She got up and stood in the veranda, at the top of the stairs leading to the garden. She liked looking at her garden at night, especially when the moonlight cast soft shadows on everything. Her flowers, her stone carvings, the lotus pond took on a subdued, elegant sheen on

these nights. There was a soft breeze playing around in the trees, teasing the leaves. It was still cool after the rain. It could get quite nippy in the evenings this time of the year. Winter in the southern hemisphere, the locals would explain. Of course, the island was only marginally affected by that winter but nevertheless there was a definite chill in the air by tropical standards. It was hard to imagine that people back home would now be dealing with the sweltering heat and humidity of the summer up north. And she was somewhere in between. Neither here nor there.

She moved back into her living room. She didn't like these moments when she felt disconcerted. It wasn't as if there was anything tangible that made her feel out of sorts. She had almost everything she wanted in life. Perhaps it was some kind of strange tropical malaise. Taking off her gold slippers, she reclined on her chaise longue. It was getting late. She filled up her glass with more wine and took another sip; this time, none too daintily. It was almost a gulp really. She turned up the volume of the music with the remote control. Was it Vivaldi now? She never used to like classical music, preferring the popular ballads of her day when she was younger. But she found the music of the great composers very soothing nowadays. None of that *gamelan* music for her. Too shrill and discordant for her ears.

She got up with some difficulty. Inertia set in so quickly on this island, especially in this quiet hamlet. She had tossed her shoes somewhere under one of the sofa chairs. She wished she could jump into her car and drive off into the night. It would be a refreshing change of pace from her solitary sequesters after dinner. When she had first got here she had made Wayan drive her to the café where they sometimes had live music – salsa, blues,

jazz – but the merry-making antics of those on vacation just filled her with equal measure of dismay and distaste.

Once there was a bohemian-looking woman who danced with such wild abandon, with frantic arm gesticulations and frenzied spinning like a dervish on amphetamines. Caroline was transfixed – she was repulsed but her eyes sought the spectacle as if it was her last sight on earth. Then there were always those lonely women of her age: making fools of themselves with their local escorts. Handsome, strapping young men fulfilling these women's every wish. For a fee, of course. It was a cheerless cliché that struck a nerve deep within her.

No, she had no stomach for such places any more. She would rather spend her evenings at home, listening to her music. Sometimes reading. Or catching up on letters or her journal-writing. A leisurely drive would have been nice but she knew there would be nothing for her to see. The streets would be deserted. The townspeople retired early for the night. Almost all of the shops and restaurants would be closed except for a few drinking holes where the resident alcoholics would be perched precariously on their barstools. Or on one of those hard benches, wedged uncomfortably next to someone reeking of stale sweat and a surfeit of booze. She couldn't quite manage that yet, to walk into one of those places alone and just strike up a conversation with a total stranger. One would have to chat about the most inane subjects and feign interest night after night. That kind of conduct was impossible for her – it was akin to being forced to learn a difficult language one day and then being expected to speak it with great fluency the very next day. She didn't know how to do it and she just couldn't be bothered to even attempt it.

* * *

She woke up with a shiver. A draught was blowing in from outside. She struggled to get up to close the doors to the veranda and she grabbed her Kashmiri throw-blanket to cover herself. One more glass of wine and that should do for the night. Her chill-blains were acting up again. She rubbed some liniment onto her knees and ankles. The years had definitely caught up with her. She wasn't as supple and agile as she once used to be.

She wondered what those women and their escorts were doing now. Would they share the same bed after a night out? How would the women undress in front of the boys? What would those boys think when they saw or touched the wrinkled skin and sagging flesh? That would have been her mortal shame. There could be little pleasure for her after such divulgence. Caroline cringed as she took another swig of Chardonnay.

She reached for her mobile phone and scrolled for Geraldine's number. Geraldine, her thirty-four-year-old niece – her favourite – was nursing a broken heart after her boyfriend of five years had run off with some trollop from his office. Poor, poor girl! The more things change, the more they stay the same. Her beloved niece had written to her asking if she could visit for a fortnight just to get away from everything. Well, they would have a grand time together. She had already worked out a comprehensive itinerary crammed with sightseeing, shopping and spas. The deluxe Bali experience. Geraldine would have no time to pine for that stupid, weak man. No time at all.

EARLY BIRD SPECIAL

In his opinion, there were only two kinds of people in Bali. The ones who belonged and those who didn't. Among the ones who didn't were the parvenus, the newcomers. These included the ones desperately seeking to be more native than the Balinese, and to be more entrenched than the so-called *bule aga*s, the pioneer Caucasians: the lucky ones who got to Bali before the onslaught of drunken weekend surfers, cheap package tours, high-decibel dance clubs and the contagion of villa developments.

The newcomers were the most bothersome. Many of them coveted what the locals and early settlers possessed; they tried too hard to be accepted by everyone until no one could bear to have them around. But this being Bali, it was customary to be tolerant and hospitable even to your worst enemy. (Or at the least one learnt to maintain a façade of tolerance.) He, Kevin Artemis Reynolds, belonged. This fact was not subject to debate. He had been living on the island for thirty years and almost everyone knew his name, his work and his face.

When he first set foot in Bali he was a young man in search of his destiny. He had sold everything off to pay for his rite of passage, a trip around the world, bolstered of course by a small stipend from his trust fund. He was just out of graduate school. He started off from the safety of Northern Europe, crossing the Mediterranean, down to hashish-infused North Africa where

the hippies were having their last hurrah, and then all the way traversing the Sahara over to Egypt. There in the shadows of the great pyramids, he planned the next leg of his trip, to Ethiopia to see the home of Haile Selassie – a sort of homage to the man Jamaican Rastafarians worshipped – but civil war and famine made the trip next to impossible. And so he decided to take the next flight out to India instead. He landed in New Delhi, and then moved on to Rajasthan. He made his way south down to Goa where he spent sun-soaked days stoked by potent ganja and zipless sex.

He thought Southeast Asia would be a fitting next destination. He found himself in Thailand and made his way through Peninsular Malaysia to Singapore. There he boarded a ship headed for Bali. And so he arrived at the port town of Singaraja. That was in 1977. He felt such a connection to the land and its people that he decided Bali would be the place he would come back to; in which to spend his old age, and bide his time until he met his Maker. He felt there was symmetry and beauty in the Balinese Hindu practice of cremations, leaving ample space for those still alive to carry on with the business of living.

He spent two ecstatic months travelling around the island on a rusty old Triumph. He had been exploring the world for a year and a half until then. His trust fund hung in the balance; after all he was supposed to be gone only for six months. He was summoned home on the threat of being disowned. And so he returned, the prodigal son – his hair had grown half way down his back – clutching his dirty rucksack filled with his treasured belongings, all faded, torn and worn from his inter-continental adventures.

In the end he lost it all anyway. His act of filial piety didn't last very long. When he told his father that he wanted no part of the financial world and that he preferred to work in international development, he was met with stone cold fury. Their agreement was that he would have his little jaunt around the world before settling down to a life of respectability. As an investment banker. After all that was the family business and it was his legacy and responsibility as the only son. His father never spoke to him again. And the trust fund was kept out of his reach for good.

By default, his destiny for the next decade was Africa but he was an abysmal failure as an aid worker. He couldn't keep sufficiently detached from the hardship and misery he saw all around him. It made him crazed with despair. He picked up several bad habits from a number of these postings. His drug and alcohol dependency for starters. And his penchant for starting bar-room brawls in the shadiest part of some disreputable African town was another. His inability to hold on to any posting for too long came soon after.

And so he drifted along in a booze-and-drug-induced cloud, barely functioning between hangovers. He got married twice during the course of that decade. The first time to a well-meaning aid worker from Norway and then to a beautiful African girl who worked at one of the bars he frequented. Both ended in hostility. It made him hate Africa more than he already did. He made a decision to get as far away from the continent as he could and that was how he ended up in Bali again. He had his severance pay in his pocket and he was hopeful that he would be able to turn his life around on the island. It was his last hope.

He spent the first few months drunk. Most mornings he

ended up unconscious on Kuta beach. He had discovered the wonders of the local brew, a palm toddy they called *arak* and he was grateful for how cheap and abundant it was. He made firm friends on the beach. From the sun-baked, chocolate boys, who taught him how to surf, to the more diligent ones who tried to arouse the entrepreneurial spirit in him by asking him to buy or sell the cheap handicrafts and batiks they were trying to unload on unwitting tourists. He tried his hand at business but he had no patience with retail. His calling was, surprisingly, teaching. He taught English to enterprising locals wanting to make a better connection with the thousands of tourists and business people who landed on the island. But he didn't charge any of the Balinese children who had found their way to him: he always made time to impart better English grammar and pronunciation to the young ones.

After five years of trying to find a balance between extended drunken sprees and living the life of his alter ego, Pak Kev, the selfless teacher, he gave it all up. He quit drinking and he quit teaching. A friend from home, Chip, another trust fund exile, wanted to start up a small hotel away from Kuta's madding crowd. He had found the ideal location tucked away in the hills of Ubud and he needed a partner who knew the local customs and language. And that was when Kevin began his stint as hotelier. Hotel Anugerah was built over a tranquil river gorge and it was the perfect place for him to rehearse his new-found sobriety. He lived the life of a monk that first year while Chip went through a steady procession of girls, local and foreign – Chip, as he proudly proclaimed, was an equal opportunity fornicator.

Kevin decided the place was good for his soul after he made

it through the worst of his withdrawal symptoms: from the drugs and alcohol chiefly but also from the friendlier, more permissive norms of Kuta and its inhabitants. Ubud was not as welcoming as Kuta; instead it was beset with cliques identified by their varying degrees of prestige within the community. As recent arrivals, Chip and he were somewhere on the periphery, a sort of social purgatory they had to endure before being decreed eligible for one of the more hallowed circles of the hamlet.

But he paid his dues over time. He was warmly received into the town's most esteemed company. His acceptance was of course commensurate with the amount of money he had accumulated. But Chip was not as lucky. He had gotten his young maid pregnant and then he wanted no part of the parenting. This earned him an instant ticket to perdition. Ostracised, Chip moved to Sanur, tail between the legs, where he continued his favourite pastime with the ladies. The pregnant girl was married off to a suitable partner who didn't question the child's parentage.

Kevin decided to buy over Chip's share and run the hotel on his own. He even expanded his little business empire to add a small bistro and a curio shop on the bustling Monkey Forest Road. He had the occasional lover but he jealously guarded his status as a single man. He had heard there was gossip that he was actually homosexual and that the girls were merely a smokescreen for the boys he took home each night. He had a feeling the rumour was started by a group of single women (mostly divorcees) from the area who were peeved that he didn't succumb to their feminine wiles. They tried hard to get his attention but he wasn't interested. They decided there was something wrong with him. He was after all an immensely eligible man of more than adequate means.

But the truth was he had found something more rewarding than the company of a woman. He had found God. It wasn't actually God in the Judeo-Christian sense of the word or anything related to the Balinese pantheon, but it had to do with an awakening and renewal of the spirit that came from having enough time to ruminate and having no worries about survival. It was the spirituality of the contented and the blessed. It was the spirituality of being able to hire enough people under you so that you could knock off early from work and disappear to practice yoga and meditation for as long as you wanted.

Meditation gave him bliss that surpassed the highs he used to get from his favourite drugs or alcohol. It was superior because there was no gut-wrenching hangover afterwards. It didn't make him frail in body or mind. It strengthened him even as he found himself steadily dependent on his daily sessions. His perceptions moved inwards, blocking out all the pettiness, all the disruption and deceit of normal human interaction. He discovered a rapture that was the closest he would ever get to the divine, as nebulous as the concept was to him. He grew less and less reliant on social interaction as he continually increased his meditation practice. He was inexorably hooked.

But just to make sure that he wasn't losing his mind, he tried connecting with other yoga and meditation groups. And so he would trudge through these classes but they always left him feeling like such an interloper. He didn't belong with them at all. They were mostly women who were too keen to share their pain or divulge what the path of enlightenment meant to them. Ad nauseam. Everything would start innocently enough, a friendly smile as someone was rolling up their yoga mat and then a

casual invitation to have a chai latte or a mango *lassi*. Then the avalanche of words. It wasn't that he thought they were padding the truth; he knew the emotions behind the stories were genuine but it just made him feel awkward and feeble. Especially when it was his turn to share. There was no way he would trivialise his very private, very wondrous experience by saying it out loud in public.

Instead of incurring the resentment of these women, they began to like him even more. To them, he was a great listener, endowed with a skill so obviously lacking in too many men. They also liked him because he was such an enigma. No one could put a finger on what he was all about. He had disclosed so very little about himself but they liked the way he was riveted by every word they said, always with his one hand cupping his face in rapt attention. But of course they never did see his other hand under the table and how he dug his fingernails into his palm until it bled.

He couldn't wait to get away from these sessions. They grated on his senses but decorum required that he sit through their chatter until everyone was done. Soon after, he stopped going to the yoga and meditation classes preferring instead to cloister himself behind the four walls of his compound. It was only in the safety and quiet of his own home that he was able to commune with the sacred. But escape wasn't to be easy. They came looking for him at his hotel, bistro and shop. When they were unsuccessful at the three locations, they appeared at the doorstep of his home, smiling widely, in anticipation of a chat and a drink.

And that was how he started his life as the accidental meditation guru. When they came to his door he felt obliged to invite them in but instead of subjecting himself to endless babbling

about their emotional pain and spiritual journey, he invited them to meditate with him. In silence. Two or three quickly became four and then five. Then they would invite other people they knew and before he could say 'Enough!' there were almost fifty people in attendance, sometimes more. Someone kindly suggested a donation box for their host to pay for the space and refreshments and before he knew it he began to amass a sizeable collection from each session.

He didn't need the money of course. The names of his hotel, the bistro and curio shop were by now established enough to make their way into the leading Bali guidebooks on which tourists were so reliant. He already had a steady stream of customers who ensured that he could live very comfortably, supported by a retinue of employees. Plus he had just started a very lucrative business of exporting wooden Christmas decorations and toys to Europe. So, he gave all the money collected from the meditation group (in addition to his own contribution) to a young Balinese who was conducting English classes for children in the area; the money was meant for books and other teaching material. He didn't tell the meditation group about these contributions but Ubud being such a rustic little hamlet, all and sundry soon learnt of his largesse.

He disliked the attention he received for his generosity. It embarrassed him acutely. He preferred to let his various kindnesses slide by unnoticed by the populace. It was a private matter much like his spirituality. But more than anything else, he disliked it being made known because it brought him into closer orbit with all the irksome newcomers. The ones with all their pushy friendliness and brash familiarity. The ones who fawned and gushed over him endlessly. The ones who didn't know him but

would invite him to their homes or hotels for a drink, or a meal as if he was by extension, because of his small-town personage, also public property.

He bore it all in silence for a time before fate intervened with a solution. Albeit one that made him suffer many more sleepless nights and troubled days. And that solution came in the form of a newcomer by the name of Sri Moksa, who was, once upon a time, born Mick Callahan. Sri Moksa was the epitome of re-invention. He had several identities over the last two decades, spanning a few continents. In his latest incarnation, he was a spiritual guru, the man who claimed that he could lead all his disciples to life-transforming epiphanies. He held the attention of his audience with his commanding presence and his oratory skills. And of course no one could deny that at forty-five, he was a very attractive and virile man. Despite his noble pretensions he was not above receiving, quite openly, gifts of money and sexual favours from his followers and admirers. So both men and women flocked to his house day and night hoping for ecstasy of one form or another.

At first Kevin was relieved that Sri Moksa had set up his operations in town. For the first time in a long time, he was able to have less intrusion and more privacy. There was a discernible decrease in invitations from strangers and less people were coming to his house for the meditation sessions. He was delighted for the peace and quiet it afforded him. But Sri Moksa found reasons to hate Kevin. Perhaps he had heard that Kevin perceived all newcomers as suspect until proven otherwise. Plus Kevin's breeding and wealth seemed to add to Sri Moksa's envy and antipathy. After all he had to depend on the generosity of

his devotees for his survival whilst Kevin owned an ever-growing portfolio of investments and assets. And so Sri Moksa went out of his way to cast aspersions on Kevin, his meditation group, his businesses and his associates.

Sri Moksa began telling his group that Kevin Artemis Reynolds was a spiritual fraud, that he was actually no closer to his salvation than the mangy dogs that roamed the streets of Bali. Plus, Sri Moksa intoned, to hope for enlightenment under such a master was the height of self-delusion and that they should stop going to Kevin's house for those silly meditation sessions where no lessons could be gleaned. Kevin's spiritual practice through the years compelled him to take a tolerant stance. The old Kev would have gone straight to Sri Moksa's house and pounded some sense into the lying bastard's head. There were still some moments when he felt like kicking the newcomer straight into the rice fields, landing him right in the midst of the mud and squawking ducks. But he was a different man now. He had to believe that in the end truth would prevail.

Once Kevin sneaked into Sri Moksa's ashram to listen to the man. He needed to know what was so fascinating about his sermons. It was common knowledge that Sri Moksa was not an ascetic; he lived lavishly and lasciviously, even as he spoke against greed and exploitation by people like Kevin. Kevin wanted to find out just how far people were being led astray by this devious newcomer. In fury, Sri Moksa denounced what he called spiritually bankrupt humanity. He railed against the stranglehold the privileged few had on the community and how there was a need for liberation of the spirit.

Kevin was perplexed: weren't New Age spiritual gurus

supposed to be preaching equanimity, compassion and tolerance? But the audience was enthralled. Then they were told to sit in silence and contemplate the import of his message. And so they meditated. To counter the vitriol of his words in the first part of his sermon, Sri Moksa ended his sermon by declaring that the answer was love, and that only love would cure all which ails the human spirit. Then in that spirit of universal love Sri Moksa asked everyone in the room to hug each other; of course, he selected the most buxom of the attendees to give one of his special extended embraces.

That night Kevin left the ashram experiencing a disturbing mix of awe and trepidation. He was certain Sri Moksa was a madman, a megalomaniac who had no concern over the community save for his own selfish interests. But there was no good way he could tell any of the man's neophytes to beware. They were still basking in the glow of Sri Moksa's words. They were mesmerised by his persona and misled by the sheer showmanship. Kevin decided to take a step back. He retreated into the safety of his business pursuits.

What was not known to many newcomers was how ably the ancient hills of Ubud healed all maladies. Since time immemorial sages and saints had come to ponder and tap into the intersection of magic and belief of the place. The hills had an uncanny way of restoring balance when things were amiss. Kevin liked to think this was why and how Sri Moksa disappeared one fateful night.

The younger man had been increasing his offensive against other so-called spiritual frauds. He said all organised religions were untruths. All spiritual leaders except him were inherently evil. And that there was only one truth, and that truth was Sri

Moksa's. His ashram had been collecting money to build new facilities in Payangan. They were planning to construct a huge complex to house a bigger lecture hall, residences and even a health retreat. They had had almost enough money to begin ground-breaking.

And then the man who was supposed to make it all happen mysteriously disappeared one rainy night. But the even bigger mystery was that Sri Moksa didn't abscond with any of the funds he had collected. He had left the money and all his other gifts behind. And it was obvious that he had left in a great hurry. It was baffling even to his closest associates and his current lovers. Kevin suspected that the man's shady past had finally caught up with him. Old sins really did have long shadows.

Life went back to normal after that. More newcomers appeared in the hills. They arrived and they left. Some stayed on. Some came looking for calm and quiet in a world they thought had gone mad; while others searched for inner peace they would never find no matter where they looked on this earth. Kevin swore off his role as meditation guru despite the pleas of his former group members. He explained that he had given up all spiritual pursuits for the simple love of making a fortune. And that seemed to be enough of an answer for all of them.

But when he was alone, in the privacy and safety of his home, he would sit in silence and let his soul reach out for the divine. For him, this was always the best reward of belonging.

MANGO SEASON

She couldn't keep her eyes away. Each time her gaze kept drifting back to the couple. The man was young, muscular, brown and pony-tailed. The woman, middle-aged, her greying blonde hair bleached almost white by the sun, and skin weather-beaten and wrinkled by the elements. Their child was in a stroller, finicky and fretting. The woman cooed at the baby, making soothing noises to placate it. When it was obvious her efforts were futile, the man stepped in, consoling it in a language she believed to be Indonesian, perhaps it was Javanese or Balinese. He looked almost half his wife's age and she had to steel her expression so that her look of disapproval wouldn't be so obvious.

The couple stood out next to the sleek European travellers in their shiny leather coats and matching designer suitcases. She wondered how they met. She wondered if either of them knew the amount of attention and scrutiny they invited as they boarded the flight. She winced, imagining herself in the woman's position: so vulnerable to all the open curiosity and the critical appraisals despite their observers' feeble attempts at being discreet.

She quickly looked down at her hands when the blonde woman reciprocated with a frank, challenging stare. It was the first time she noticed how wrinkled and frail her own hands were, as if denuded by the absence of the wedding band that had been there for seventeen years. She shook her head, mentally reminding

herself that she would never sink so low as to seduce a boy young enough to be her son, much less let him father her child. She would never allow herself to be that lonely and desperate. Never, she vowed.

* * *

Her third day in paradise and she was feeling alone and bereft. That hollow pain in her chest was almost palpable. She was having her breakfast at her usual spot on Double 6, an unassuming little café overlooking the waves pounding on the beige sand. On the beach, there were people walking along listlessly, clutching their shoes and flip-flops, some young couples were strolling hand in hand while scores of skinny stray dogs chased each other maniacally up and down the sand. It was still too early for the petty traders and the burnt chocolate beach boys to be out, begging and hustling tourists to part with some holiday rupiahs.

She tried to practice a smile, just anything to conceal her sense of dread and remorse, that this vacation, her dream trip to Bali, was yet another colossal mistake. Another error in judgement, among the many, she had chalked up since the divorce. She flicked back a stray auburn curl loosened by a strong gust from the sea and then she gestured to the waiter for another coffee. She noticed him then, a young local man, watching her intently. He gave her a lopsided grin when he caught her eye. She could only glare at him for his audacity. A pick-up attempt at 9 am? Only in Bali, she thought, shaking her head. This was exactly what some of her friends back home had warned her about.

She shifted her body in the chair ever so slightly so that he

wasn't in her line of sight any more. Who does he think she is? Some desperate, bored woman in search of mindless excitement? God knows who he's been with. She shook her head in disbelief. She sipped her coffee slowly, mentally charting her day. The last few days she had passed the time by browsing in all the small shops in Kuta, followed by sunning and reading by the pool or long massage sessions at the hotel.

Shopping, once her favourite pastime, now filled her with anxiety. She had been chased up and down the block and then all the way to the strip of Kuta beach by the street peddlers who were frantically plying everything from manicures and pedicures, braids, massage and cheap costume jewellery. She felt exhausted each time one of them came up to her begging and cajoling her to try something, buy something. Help me out please, they pleaded. It made her feel selfish and raw and ugly. Like carrion tossed amidst a pack of hungry hyenas.

'You here alone?' said a gravelly voice with a trace of Australian accent. It startled her, left her speechless. She nodded unsmilingly at the young Indonesian who had been staring at her. He was taller than average with a very straight carriage. He had short hair, a small silver-ring in his ear. He was a deep dark brown from the sun and his straight white teeth flashed bright in contrast. He bore his good looks with easy confidence.

'Do you want some company? You look sad,' he persisted.

She had to clear her throat, a moment to regain her composure.

'I'm sorry. I'm ... ahh ... just ... just trying to enjoy my breakfast and the view ...' she gestured expansively at the seafront, as words failed her again.

'Well, I don't like to eat alone. I could use some company.

How about it?' He said as he sat himself in a chair opposite her.

She gasped in disbelief and relented. 'Suit yourself,' she shot back, not wanting to make a scene amidst the sedate breakfast crowd, most of whom appeared to be regulars.

Surprisingly he was quiet. He took out a cigarette and when he determined that she didn't mind, he smoked in pensive silence. When he was done with the cigarette, he drank his coffee and shifted his attention to her, scrutinizing her face, her hands, her neck, her breasts unabashedly.

'Excuse me?' she demanded.

'For what? Did you do something wrong?' he asked, in a tone of amused curiosity.

'Where I come from it's rude to stare like that,' she hissed.

'I think it's rude to speak to someone who obviously doesn't want conversation,' he smiled rakishly, putting on the charm again.

She sighed. 'Look, I don't know what kind of woman you think I am but I'm not interested in anything you're selling. I'm just trying to ... to have a good time on my holiday.'

'You don't have a very high opinion of people, and of yourself, do you?' he smiled, now assessing her even more closely.

'Pardon?' she said, narrowing her eyes.

'Look, I just don't like to be alone. You're an attractive woman sitting alone, who looks not so happy. So I thought I was doing both of us a favour. Nothing more. It's just breakfast. Don't freak out,' he said tiredly.

'I'm not freaking out. I am not the kind of person who freaks out.' She inched closer to him as she spat the words out.

'Then prove it. Besides, what on earth could I do to you here,

with all these people around us? Rape you? Rob you? I come here all the time. People know me.'

She just stared at him, wide-eyed. She was amazed at how self-assured he was despite his young age.

'And why would I need to use force to take something that's always given to me for free?' he added, as he settled himself into a more comfortable position in the chair.

*　*　*

She marvelled at his demeanour all through breakfast. Gone was his bravado and almost predatory posturing that had made her hackles rise. He was quiet, polite and attentive. When she relaxed, she found herself grateful for the company of another human after the three lonely days of navigating the streets and beaches of Kuta and Seminyak alone. He didn't try to conceal the fact that he found her attractive but there was no attempt to flatter her into submission, as she had feared.

When he told her that he had to rush off for another appointment she was disappointed. He shook her hand with a firm grip, and told her that he hoped that he would run into her again. She just smiled and nodded wordlessly, still uncertain as to how she should handle the attention. She looked around her suddenly feeling self-conscious about her breakfast encounter and her easy assent to his company, wondering if anyone on the other tables was looking at her, if anyone was judging her the way she did the couple at the airport.

She sat by herself at the table for about fifteen minutes before

deciding to go back to her hotel to read by the pool and then go for a massage. She fiddled nervously with the keys to her villa at the resort, trying hard to act nonchalantly as she sauntered to the entrance of the eatery. Everyone else seemed to be preoccupied with their breakfast, some gazing out to the seafront while others were chatting amiably with their family or companions. She felt conspicuously alone.

She was grateful that Nyoman, her masseuse, was not a chatty girl. She slid onto the massage bed naked and Nyoman went to work on her immediately, starting with her feet and working up her calves and thighs to the rest of her body. These extended massage sessions were a sensual experience that left her breathless in gratitude. It made her aware of just how much her body had been craving for human touch and this realisation was mortifying to her.

Three days ago, the very first time Nyoman had touched her – slathering oil on her body and expertly pressing away the kinks and knots of tension in her neck, her back, her buttocks –- she started crying soundlessly. She remembered how her tears dropped through the aperture of the massage bed straight down to the floor, into the wooden bowl filled with frangipanis and scarlet hibiscus. Her tears were like a silent offering, landing delicately on the velvet white petals of the fragrant frangipani.

*   *   *

It was dusk when she woke up from her nap. Long shadows filled the room and the fading red gold sunlight streamed in through the veranda. Sounds of the *gamelan* drifted gently from the lobby

into her room with the evening breeze. Waking up each morning was easy enough, there was always the anticipation of what the new day had to offer. New people, new sights, new sensations that came from being the lone traveller in a place visited for the very first time. But facing the end of another day left her with a melancholic ache that made her crave for the salve of human company. Just anyone to talk to, just anyone to remind her, to help her bear witness that her presence here on this earth meant something, that it wasn't just some accident of fate.

Her life back home seemed like light years away. The warm tropical island, the lush green villa were a safe haven from the stony silences with Jim. He was probably still sorting out his possessions at the home they had shared for fifteen years. She could imagine him painstakingly picking out the CDs that would go with him to his swanky new duplex. She told him that he could take anything he wanted from the house. Her friends and sister had scolded her for her generosity but she knew Jim's sense of fair-play would mean that he would spend hours just making sure that her favourite CDs and books, for that matter any of their shared prized possessions would remain with her. But she knew it was also his act of contrition for no longer needing her, for wanting to start a brand new life without her.

There was no other woman or man, only between them, a diminution of love and lust for each other that played out in longer hours spent at work and even longer silences when they were together. They had ceased having passion for their life together. The future loomed large as one endless life sentence together. No matter how many times they tried to resuscitate their marriage, they failed to revive the warmth and appreciation that

they once had for one another. Perhaps the absence of children hastened the decline but it just made their emotional distance even more excruciating. Once all they had in the world was each other and they clung on like two shipwrecked survivors on a life raft. Making love was always tinged with desperate ferocity that left them gasping, hungry for more each time.

Towards the end, they could scarcely bear to touch even if it was by accident. They would lie, each sequestered by their books, pillows and cushions, on opposite sides of the king-sized bed, sometimes feigning sleep by regulating their breathing as if in deep slumber, just to avoid having to speak to one another. Resentment and uncertainty left them wide awake through most nights. More than once she had spied Jim quietly pleasuring himself under the bedclothes. He was touching, stroking himself, his eyes squeezed shut in pained concentration and when that did not work he would quietly rub himself against the soft sheets until he reached a shuddering climax.

She was filled with both remorse and revulsion on those occasions. She hated him for not reaching out to her first and she hated herself for her own mute acceptance. But she knew she would have probably recoiled in disgust had he sought her in the middle of the night, because all desire for him had long dissipated. She had ceased to think of herself as a woman worthy of any man's attention. Desire had become risky and unreliable and it had no place in her life. Even her clothes began to reflect this as she opted for turtleneck sweaters and baggy pants, anything that would aid in concealing any hint of femininity, any trace of sexuality.

Shadows suffused the room and the night arrived quickly.

Someone had switched on the small lamps in the private garden of her villa. Outside, the cicadas struck up a spirited chorus, almost challenging the soft strains of *gamelan* music. She got up slowly, in semi stupor from her long nap. She took off her robe and prepared for her bath. She lit candles all around her open-air bathroom. The bathtub was under the stars, surrounded by lush tropical palms and plants with fragrant blossoms. She poured the bath oil into the tub and climbed into the tepid water. She gasped at the sheer sensual pleasure of the experience. She slid herself lower into the water, submerging her neck and chin until it lapped up to her lower lip. It felt as if every inch of her body needed this.

Not ten minutes had passed and suddenly she sat up, shaking her head as she climbed out of the tub. She reached for her towel, gave her body a brisk drying and then her hair, bundling it all up into a turban with the towel. She stood naked in front of the full-length mirror in the bedroom, as she applied lotion to her still damp skin. She started off with her arms, now golden brown from the strong Bali sun. She slowly rubbed the lotion into her neck down to her upper chest before lingering slowly on her breasts. Her breasts were still full and firm at forty-seven. Her stomach was flat and her thighs trim from the running that she did religiously every morning.

She smoothed the lotion on her lower stomach, down to her thighs. She moved up her inner thighs till she reached between her legs where she remained. She covered her pubic area with her hand like it was a fig leaf. She stared hard at the tanned naked stranger in the mirror, a wary interloper with green eyes that gleamed with questions. Almost as an afterthought she touched herself, furtively at first, then stroking softly underneath, working

through with increasing pressure on her most sensitive parts until she felt a frisson of pleasure suffuse her entire body. She continued to steal peeks at herself in the mirror and it aroused her even more. The naked stranger stared back at her almost defiantly, her nipples now hard, her whole body taut with anticipation.

A small sigh of ecstasy escaped her lips as she went deeper, delving with more momentum, pushing her toward closer to delirium. The stranger in the mirror was now writhing and groaning with primal abandon. Her climax brought her to her knees and she fell to the floor in a quivering heap of limbs. As the tingling waves of sensation diminished all she could feel was an immense emptiness. It was eerily silent and then the rain came, pouring down in sheets of quicksilver. The deluge drenched the bathroom, drowning out the candles, flattening the palm fronds and pounding on the flowers vengefully. She curled herself up in a semi-foetal position on the bedroom floor, looking out at the rain, holding tightly onto the towel as if it was a security blanket. Her tears come in torrents. For the first time since the divorce she cried, her sobs rocking her whole body. She wept for all that was lost as the thunderstorm surged outside.

* * *

The inhabitants of the island were early risers. It was only seven thirty in the morning and most of the staff of the resort had already been at work for more than an hour. The aftermath of last night's thunderstorm had been dealt with quickly and efficiently. The broken branches, fallen leaves and flowers had already been swept aside and placed into neat piles in the corner of the garden.

The gardener was still working at the plunge pool, scooping out the leaves and other debris from the water. At the corner of the garden, someone had already placed the first of the day's offerings on the altar of the villa's temple, the smoke from the incense floated up to the heavens to venerate the Gods.

She grabbed her hat, sunglasses and handbag, ready to head for her usual breakfast spot by the beach. She waved at the gardener and bade him a quick greeting. He gestured to the pavilion next to the plunge pool. She noticed the basket of mangoes at the centre of the pavilion's wooden platform. The gardener told her that a man had dropped them off for her about an hour ago. She took the basket, wondering who could have given her the luscious fruit. She loved mangoes and these looked ripe enough to be eaten immediately. She had seen scores of mango trees around the houses nearby, their branches heavily laden with the ripe fruit, just waiting to be plucked. She left the fruit in the house, pleased at her early morning gift – the mere thought of sinking her teeth into the plump, juicy flesh of the mangoes made her smile. There was a newfound spring to her step as she walked to the café for her breakfast. It was funny how a simple basket of fruit could erase last night's despair. Definitely cheaper than a psychiatrist, she grinned.

She stopped by the beach for a closer look at the sea. The beach-combers were out in full force, accompanied by the over-active dogs and their usual tail-chasing antics. It was low tide and the surf was some distance away from the beach this morning. The small crabs were already busy tunnelling their way to the surface to get some heat and sustenance from the beach, their efforts leaving distinctive dots and spirals on the wet sand. Her

worries, her tears last night seemed like a hundred lifetimes away with the sunshine and sea breeze. She took a deep breath, drawing in the sweet scent of the sea.

'You look like a different person,' a voice greeted her.

'What? Oh, it's you.' She looked around to see the young man from the other day, her less than welcomed breakfast companion. He looked even younger today, clad in a damp T-shirt, and a pair of knee-length surfer shorts festooned with the motif of red frangipanis.

'So what were you thinking about? Happy thoughts? You were actually smiling and not scowling at the world.'

She nodded.

'I hope your good mood has something to do with my mangoes.'

'Your mangoes? Those were from you? How did you know where I was staying?'

'This is my territory. I have eyes and ears everywhere. Have you eaten any of the mangoes? They're very special, you know,' he said to her teasingly. 'Plus I believe it's customary for your people to say thank you when given a present?'

'Thank you. It was very kind of you. No, no I haven't eaten any of your mangoes yet. And why are they so special?'

'They came from my father's garden. He's usually very stingy with his mangoes,' he shrugged.

'Well, I'm honoured then … Look … I'm going to have breakfast, would … would you … like to have some coffee?'

'Only coffee for my father's prized mangoes? Madam, you're buying me breakfast,' he said as he took her arm gently and led her to the café.

His name was Wayan Suena and he was thirty-three. His fluent English and self-assuredness came from years of dealing with tourists, mostly surfers, he said. And of course the many girls he dated, including the Australian with whom he fathered a child, married, moved to Perth, left Perth and then divorced – in that order. His ex-wife was six years older than him, and she very much wanted that baby and as it turned out, he explained, more than she ever wanted him. Which was why he had come back to Bali, he said. He told her all without a trace of self-pity or bitterness. He was now helping his father manage the family property: land which had been built up with houses and shops that were rented out to tourists and frequent visitors who wanted a bigger slice of paradise. It was a good living, he said, even though things had been a bit slow since the bombings.

When it was her turn to reciprocate with a few personal details about herself, she found that she couldn't. She sat next to him, tongue-tied, looking at the waves and the increased activity on the beach until the silence changed from companionable to uncomfortable. He finally broke the silence by taking hold of her hand and squeezing it lightly.

'Hey, the least you can do is to tell me your name – I mean what your friends and family call you. I already know your last name, Mrs Cross. I think that name suits you very well.'

She smiled in spite of herself, 'My name is Suzanne. And my friends call me Sue. I'm divorced, so technically I'm no longer Mrs anything. It's back to Sue Williams.'

'Sue. Sweet, sweet Sue. It's okay, Sue,' He touched the back of her hand lightly, lit one of his unfiltered clove cigarettes, and looked out onto the surf, deep in thought. She inhaled the

heady scent of his cigarettes, feeling the most alive she had ever been in weeks.

The shrill ringing of his mobile phone ended their reverie. He answered his caller in English. Smiling, he stood up and walked to the entrance of the eatery to continue his conversation outside. Then his posture changed from relaxed to tense in just a matter of minutes. The call ended abruptly and he came back to the table looking sombre.

'Look, I've got to go. We'll meet again. Don't finish all those mangoes on your own. Promise you'll share some with me,' he said, and then as suddenly as he had appeared, he was gone.

This time she felt no discomfiture after he left. She ate her breakfast at leisure and when she was done she sauntered out of the eatery without as much as a backward glance. She hired a car and a driver at the resort and headed straight for the art galleries in Ubud, a hill town about an hour's drive away. She spent most of the day poring over paintings and sculptures by artists local and foreign and she felt a long dormant desire to paint surge within her again. She had let her artistic abilities be subsumed by her graphic design work for too long – all creative spontaneity and enthusiasm had been stifled by deadlines and her clients' demands.

* * *

It was dusk when she got back to the villa and she was tired. Her thoughts kept going back to him. What would Wayan be doing now and with whom? But she didn't want to allow herself too much time mulling over him. It was a humid night with a weak,

low breeze that scarcely made the air move within the four high walls of her garden. She stripped down to her underwear and sat in her pavilion slowly sipping her drink as the night engulfed her. When her drink was finished she took off her bra and panties, folded them neatly on a patio table, and jumped feet first into the plunge pool. She yelped in surprise at the cool bite of the water but it felt good after a day of sweating it out in the hills, traipsing from one gallery to the next.

The loud knock on the heavy outer wooden doors of her walled garden startled her. She felt like a teenager caught smoking in the toilet and she quickly clambered out of the pool, running naked into the villa, leaving a watery trail behind her. She slipped into a dressing gown and ran to the door, lifting the wooden bar that lay across the intricately carved double doors. It was Wayan Suena.

'Were you asleep?' he asked as he peered into the garden, scrutinising her face, her body.

'No, not yet. What are you doing here?' She tightened the belt on the gown and brought the collar closer together to cover her chest.

'I came to eat mangoes with you. You could ask me in.'

She led him to the pavilion with a nod and told him to wait. She went into her little kitchen and brought the mangoes out on a plate with a knife. When she returned, he was smirking, holding up her bra and panties to her. Her alarmed reaction, her embarrassment at his discovery elicited a loud laugh from him. His laughter boomed across the stillness of the night like thunder.

'I was taking a dip in the pool to cool off. Alone,' she snapped at him, snatching the underwear from his grasp.

'No need to explain. Your expression was priceless. I wish I had a camera with me.'

'You know, despite your generosity, you have quite a mean streak!'

'Please don't get all uptight again. I was just teasing. Here, let me cut those mangoes for you. Come sit beside me,' he said, patting a spot close to him on the pavilion.

She sat next to him as he deftly started to peel and slice the mangoes. He proffered her a slice before eating one himself. The mango was delightfully sweet and juicy, just as she had imagined. When he was done slicing all the mangoes in neat sections, he took another piece and put it against her lips.

'Eat,' he commanded as she began to protest. He fed her as one would a baby. When she was done, he ate a slice. He did this with two more slices for her, and two for himself. He fed her a third and then he slowly leaned over to lick her lips ever so softly, flicking his tongue gently over her mouth before kissing her tenderly. She was so shocked she couldn't move and then her body responded: she returned his kiss ardently, her tongue probing deeper into his mouth to taste him.

He pushed her away gently and then he ate his slice, savouring each bite unhurriedly. She watched him bewildered. When he was done, he put another slice across her lips before trailing it down her neck very slowly, down to her breasts, encircling her nipples. She watched wide-eyed as he slipped her dressing gown down one shoulder, and like a cat, he lapped the trail of mango juice starting from her lips, down to her neck and then to her breasts. He did this with agonising deliberateness as if he didn't want to miss a single precious trace of the mango. She groaned, she slipped her

arms out of the gown's sleeves impatiently and arched her body towards him. He stopped, again pushing her away.

'I don't think we should take this any further. Not tonight. Don't you agree?' he said evenly, not a trace of arousal in his voice.

She kept silent, not knowing how to reply without losing what remaining shred of dignity she had. She felt like a gauche teenager again, just learning how to navigate the tricky emotional landscape of lust and desire. She inched away from him to widen the space between them. He was also quiet after the encounter. He lit one of his clove cigarettes and he sat in the corner of the pavilion, looking at her through the veil of pungent smoke that curled its way to her.

'Do you know how beautiful you are?' he stated, a thought thrown languidly at her as if in compensation. She just shook her head in disbelief, not merely at him but at the situation. When he was done with his cigarette, he closed the distance between them and touched her face. He traced the outline of her cheek and lips, and then he pulled her close to him. He just held her without a word. After a while, he kissed her forehead.

'I'm leaving. You have a good rest. We'll meet again,' he promised. He stood up, walked to the outer door and closed it behind him softly with one last look at her, as she sat in the shadows in the far corner of the pavilion.

* * *

She woke up to the scent of ripe mangoes and of him. She could still smell him on her skin and in her hair. She felt a ripple of

desire as she remembered their encounter last night. She had never met anyone so forthright and yet so evasive about wanting to make love to her. Well, perhaps love wasn't quite the word. It was clearly lust. Albeit lust that was kept in control. She thought of her frantic sessions as a teenager and as a student in university, clumsy couplings induced by raging hormones, excess alcohol and loneliness. Those boys were always too eager and too fast it always felt like a violation at the end. It was different with Jim, he was older and more meticulous. Lovemaking was always preceded by elaborate preparation – candles, mood music, sometimes even flowers – in comfortable rooms where they would spend a night, whole afternoons, or an entire weekend with no interruptions.

The smell of the mangoes made her mouth water. She was still naked when she got out of bed. Not bothering to put on her robe, she went to the dining area and picked the ripest mango and peeled it. And she immediately ate it like a child, letting the juice drip messily over her chin, breasts and belly. She felt delirious and recklessly young.

Her buoyant feeling carried over into the afternoon as she wandered aimlessly around Kuta looking for curios and gifts for people back home. She was quite happy spending money on silly trinkets and other strictly unnecessary souvenirs, chatting amiably with the shop assistants. When she felt tired she walked into an airy little café and ordered a cool glass of lime juice. She was leaving the café when she saw him across the street. Her first instinct was to call out his name but she noticed that he was not alone.

Wayan Suena was holding a local girl by her upper arm. The Balinese girl, who was perhaps in her early twenties, looked

visibly upset. Wayan's face was menacingly close to hers. Every so often as if to emphasise a point he would shake her arm. The girl looked at the ground, she kept nodding her head in silence as he carried on with his reprimand. He was talking in Balinese. He was too engrossed to notice her staring at them.

She walked away feeling like an interloper. She wondered who the girl could be. A lover, a relative, a friend? Why was he so angry? The bubble of contentment that carried her along all morning had disappeared. All the questions left an uneasy feeling. She felt exhausted and bewildered. Foolish, even. She went straight to her villa and dropped all her shopping on the floor. She took off her sweat sodden T-shirt and shorts and climbed into bed.

She woke up just as dusk started to fill the villa with golden copper glow. The light disoriented her and she got out of her groggily, still unsteady on her feet. The knocking on her wooden front gate didn't register immediately in her head. She was just trying to remember where she was and she felt momentarily distressed to know that she wasn't in the comforting familiarity of her bedroom, of her house. She heard her name being called then. 'Sue.' Then, louder, 'Suzanne.' She grabbed her bathrobe and stumbled through the villa to get to the gate.

Wayan Suena was leaning against outer wall when she opened the door. She didn't quite know how to react to his lopsided grin or the intimate way he tucked her stray auburn hair behind her ear. He stroked her cheek and led her through the doorway into her garden. With one hand he closed the wooden door behind him with a resounding thud. With the other he held onto her arm and still without a word of greeting, led her to her villa.

As soon as they were indoors his mouth sought hers, pushing

her robe off her shoulders and onto the floor. She went limp. She was futile against the heat of his body and his arms holding her upright. He kissed her again, tongue on tongue, as he unhooked her bra and swiftly slipped her panties past her hips and down to the ground. She felt betrayed by her body. A terrifying weakness left her depleted of any resistance. His lips strayed down to her breasts, nibbling and sucking on her nipples like a starved infant. His hands stroked and squeezed her buttocks with increasing pressure, and then they were between her legs, seeking her most tender points with expert precision. Taking off his pants, he pushed her onto the bed and started to nuzzle between her legs, teasing her with his lips from her inner thighs and probing inwards. Then with a groan he stopped and climbed on top of her and entered her with one resolute movement.

* * *

It was close to midnight when she awakened to the smell of over-ripened mangoes from the kitchen. He was asleep on his side, his back towards her, an arm tucked gracefully underneath his head in peaceful repose. He looked so young and vulnerable. There was no trace of the man whom had dominated every movement of their intercourse. Each time she had tried to assert her desire he would pull back or hold her off until he regained control. He had no need for an equal in bed. He would lead and she was to follow. He and only he was responsible for both their pleasure.

She stretched cat-like and smiled at how eagerly she had responded to him. At first she was chagrined, even angry, but she knew she was fighting a losing battle and so she just surrendered.

She had never been with a lover who was as domineering and as certain of each and every move as he. She liked that he was so uninhibited and so definite about pleasuring himself and her to the utmost of his abilities. He certainly had stamina. And finesse – a surprising delicacy of touch that took the rough edges off his aggressive ways.

She gently traced the tattoo on his shoulder. A surfer riding a massive wave. She never knew he had it. It was always concealed underneath the sleeve of his T-shirt. There was so much she didn't know about him. A stranger who had bought her affections with a mere basket of mangoes. And yet here he was in her bed. In that one night, she had allowed him to do to her what she denied her husband for years. He stirred and turned towards her. In semi-sleep, he reached out to hold her closer. He held her tightly to him as if he was scared she would run off into the night. She lay in his arms quietly, trying to breathe evenly and normally.

She thought of the girl she had seen him with. Who on earth could she be? His sister or girlfriend, of worse yet, perhaps, even wife? That would explain his proprietary behaviour towards the girl. What did the girl do wrong? She wanted to trust him but for now her questions would have to remain unspoken. It was hard for her to acknowledge this encounter for what it was, but there it was staring at her in the face: this was a tryst between a lonely woman on holiday and a local man familiar to such assignations.

He stirred again and pulled her more forcefully towards him. He started caressing her softly, and then he was fondling her with more ardour and none too gently. He stopped and embraced her closer until they were chest to chest and groin to groin. He manoeuvered on top of her until she was pinned beneath him.

He kissed her hungrily, nibbling, biting on her neck and ears until she could hear her thoughts no more. Only dark pulsating sensations of pleasure reeling her in, deeper and deeper, blocking out everything: her every thought, her every question, her every fear.

REMEMBERING

One day a memory appeared in a startling instant. A recollection of something that happened decades ago, surfaced with no reason. Something that was long buried in the recesses of his mind. It returned when he was on the veranda having a smoke, looking out at the inky darkness which was, in the light of day, golden brown rice fields waiting to be harvested. There was a delicate scent of frangipanis and ylang-ylang in the air, from the small garden on the side of the house. He remembered that her name was Teresa.

They were both sophomores in college. They would meet every so often in the library but she was nowhere to be seen for a couple of weeks, her usual spot at the table left vacant. When she reappeared, he asked her if she had been on vacation at some exotic destination. Hawaii? Jamaica? Anywhere totally different from the bleak winter netherworld that they were living in. The wind chill factor was minus twenty-five, he remembered that now. She had smiled and ever so quietly, told him that her mother had died. He could only manage an ineffectual 'Oh' and he went back to his reading, red-faced. Why would he remember Teresa now? After a lapse of forty years. They never dated. They never even had coffee or soda together in the cafeteria. She was just the curly-haired brunette he sometimes spoke to in the library. Average-looking. Immensely forgettable.

He stubbed out his cigarette and went back to his laptop in the sitting room. The ceiling fan was whirring drowsily round and round and there was a big spotted gecko peering at him from the top of the wall. He was supposed to start work on another two chapters today. Outlines of chapters really, for his next book, the one on Mongolia.

His publishing agent, Liz, had been e-mailing him these trite little reminders – her tone was torn between rueful and surly. He had replied very breezily, 'Fuck off, woman!' And as easy as that, no more annoying reminders. He had the license to do that, he had known her for almost twenty years. A volatile relationship based on mutual need and mutual vexation. But Liz had always been there for him. More loyal than most wives. Steering him onward. Dissuading him from his more lacklustre subjects to the ones she was certain would sell. And sell they did.

He had become one of the leading authors in the travelogue genre. There were so many bitter and jaded writers already starring in the best-seller lists. The ones who earned millions of dollars and accolades on the back of their cynicism and scorn. He assumed people liked his books because he never lost his sense of wonder. He was just muddling along with his curiosity; he was the ingenuous one trying to find some answers among strangers. And the fact was when he immersed himself in a place and a people, with all their peculiar rhythms and cadences, he always nailed it. People who had been to the country or the region he wrote about understood this immediately. Even the armchair travellers seemed to recognise this. And so people bought his books. From everywhere they read English, and when they didn't, his books were translated into five other languages. Liz once mentioned

gleefully that she was planning to tap into the Chinese market. He remembered how her eyes lit up over at the prospect of millions of yuan.

He'd be lying if he said he didn't like the money. The money afforded him a lifestyle that was authentically his own. He didn't care much for living large – he had never been one for the big house with a pool, or the entourage of servants and handlers or flashy cars. He lived simply and quietly, books and travel being his only extravagance. The money allowed him the latitude to do what he pleased, wherever the heck he pleased. And wherever happened to be Bali this time around, the Isle of the Gods as the tourist brochures modestly proclaimed. The place had its appeal and the novelty factor was compelling enough to keep him rooted for another couple of years. Barring any unforeseen circumstances or the sudden onset of boredom. Whichever came first.

He rode around town in a beat-up two-door jeep. He would have opted for a motorbike but the weather was too capricious in these hills. The rains came down suddenly, frequently and hard. He liked to move around with his laptop and at least a couple of books. Convenience and a matter of security. Once when he was travelling through Uzbekistan, someone stole his laptop and three months' worth of work. It was the closest he ever felt to being violated. The expensive laptop was the least of his concerns then; he feared that all his thoughts, his observations, his first impressions could never be replicated. Or so he thought. But it was easy enough to recapture the words he had committed to the computer. Once he sat down and made a concerted effort to remember, the words came back. He stumbled over the first few paragraphs and then the words started to flow, then it came back

in torrents. It was like that in the early days. Words were always faithful. Writing was his protection.

He looked at the empty page. The cursor blinked, reproachful. He had been through enough variations of the writer's block to know that something else was happening here. For days now he had been avoiding this moment by taking long drives up to the mountains and back (Kintamani, Bedugul), long coffee breaks that segued into beer drinking sessions with the town's many expatriate reprobates, or passionate chats with his Balinese friends in their homes in the village (about rituals, magic, culture, tourism, money). Or reading. And he had many books in which to lose himself. Some were research for his Mongolian book. History and social anthropology mostly, to flesh out his own observations. Others were classics. Dostoevsky. Steinbeck. Conrad.

He could never understand writers who likened writing to a marathon. They said they kept to a disciplined, well-paced daily routine that was always productive. Productive. The word always made him smile. A cough was productive when it produced phlegm. Writing was never a predictably productive exercise for him. It was reliable and he believed in it. He believed in himself when he wrote. But it didn't happen every day, every time, right on the dot. He was like a sprinter. There were short bursts of creative energy (in which he could write many chapters) followed by long periods of rest and rumination.

The sprint had been stalled for so many days now. It was as if he had lost steam in the race right after he had shot off from the starter's block. The words would flow for a few lines then he would have trouble recollecting the name of a place or a person. This wasn't really a problem because he took copious notes when

he was on the road but these days he was losing words. Simple words. Words that should have come easily without the aid of a thesaurus or additional thinking. Was he distracted about something that he didn't even dare to admit? What did he have to worry about? His sons were all grown-up. They had graduated, one was working in investment banking and the other was in futures, or was it hedge funds? In any case they were both well-adjusted, *productive* young men.

His ex-wife Gina had always been high-strung. He was drawn to her energy and her honesty from the first time he set eyes on her. She was the kind of woman who provoked ardour in everyone she met. No half-way measures for her. It was so different from everything he was used to: his parents were models of middle-class, Mid-West restraint. Good, solid citizens who loved their kids but certainly never smothered them with affection. A hand-shake or a hug from his father. A kiss on the cheek from his mother now and then. A chastise from either his father or mother usually meant silence. He couldn't really remember too much of his childhood beyond the feeling that they were good parents but careful about everything.

It started raining. A drizzle that gained strength to become a heavy downpour. He had hoped to have dinner at the popular eatery in Campuhan where the expats liked to congregate over smoky ribs and cheap beer. It was the next best thing to a family dinner for the ones in transit like him. For some of them that transit had spanned more than a few decades. Some had married locals, while others had drifted in and out of relationships, never really feeling as if they belonged in Bali. But he suspected that they probably never felt as if they belonged anywhere else.

He was preparing himself a sandwich in his cramped kitchen when he remembered a dinner at home when he was about nine or ten. His mother hadn't been talking to his father for about a week. He asked his mother but she just gave him a big unsteady smile and told him not to worry. 'It's just grown-up stuff, my dear,' was what she said, patting him on his arm gently. Dinner was always supposed to be family time – the time to catch up on everyone's day. But of course the conversation was stilted because his father and mother were still not on speaking terms. His father had tried to speak to his mother for a few days but he stopped trying after all his overtures failed to elicit any response. His brother and two sisters were seated at the table, eating quietly. All of them were anxious to finish dinner and get away as soon as they could. And then his father suddenly stood up in the middle of the meal. His first thought was that his father was going to get more water or something else from the kitchen but he just took his dinner plate, which still had quite a bit of the pot roast, vegetables and mashed potatoes, and he smashed it on the floor right next to his chair.

One abrupt movement and he had shattered the plate to smithereens. His mother had started crying and then she ran upstairs. His father went out to the back porch without a word.

He never found out why his mother didn't speak to his father. But everything went back to normal soon after that. At some point they must have made up with each other but he couldn't remember when or how they reconciled.

After his father had smashed his plate, his siblings and he didn't finish their pot roast. He remembered that he was still hungry. The meal was delicious and he wanted to continue eating but it seemed like the wrong thing to do. He remembered how

his sister, Jan, took charge by scraping everyone's plates into the trash can.

He was in front of his laptop with his sandwich. He shook his head; these surprising little detours to the past were baffling. He had always taken pride in living in the present. Travelling as frequently as he did required that state of mind. There was no room for reflection or regrets about the past. Was it this place? This house?

It had been only three months since he moved into the house. A trial period. During the day the house was usually filled with beautiful light. The golden glow from the rice fields was set off by the blue intensity of the sky. The garden was charming with its shrubbery of various fragrant blooms, a small mango tree laden with green fruit, a fishpond and the pergola. But at night it was different. It became sombre and seemed suffused with desolation. He switched on more lamps around the room and the light on the veranda; anything to dispel the sense of foreboding. Maybe it was because of all the rain lately but he felt as if the darkness was gaining ground, seeping in through the floorboards, through the cracks and crevices in the walls and ceiling.

The idea for the house was planted when he was in Bangkok last year; he had met a fellow writer who told him that in this Bali town or its many surrounding villages, one could build a nice quiet home, a retreat for writing or meditation. The Czech writer was a New Age type, prone to ethereal flights of fancy but the man was earnest and good. And he had been on the road for eighteen solid months, researching his next book and helping his publishers' peddle an earlier book on his travels in Central Asia. He was tired of hotel rooms and airports and living like an up-

market hobo. What the Czech said had intrigued him. He wanted to stay on in Southeast Asia and the timing seemed right to set up home temporarily in Bali, with the option of getting a piece of land and building his own house if things went well.

He ended up spending three days in Bangkok with the Czech. They talked about Bali and its people. Disappearing indigenous cultures. The utility and futility of organised religion. Astrology. Akashic records. Philosophy. Literature. The oil crisis. The man had some crazy ideas but his heart was in the right place. He tried to remember the Czech's name but it escaped him. Milo? Milan? No. This would never have happened in the past. He couldn't even remember how the man looked like. He was now just a hazy composite of ideas and emotions.

At 10.30 pm he was snugly tucked in bed with a book on modern Mongolian history. He was just about to doze off when his phone beeped. It was a text message from Kadek. He was probably the only Balinese in town he knew whom was still awake beyond eleven o'clock at night. As a rule the locals retired early for the night and they rose way before the crack of dawn. The circadian rhythms of farming life are so ingrained in their DNA and so hard to break; no matter if they are now hotel owners or shopkeepers or travel guides or drivers. Kadek was going to bring him to Denpasar in the morning to see a skin specialist for a rash that didn't seem to go away. It was one of his many Mongolian mementos.

He got up with a start. The clock by the bedside showed 3.43 am; his book had fallen off the bed with a thud. He picked it up off the floor and put it back by his pillow. When he was a little boy, Grandpa Joe used to have this strange habit of putting his

shoes right next to his pillow. It was just a few months before the old man died. He remembered that well because if he had done something like that his parents would have punished him. And Grandpa Joe also liked wearing two watches at the same time. Once his grandfather had touched his Mickey Mouse watch and said, 'I like your knife, who bought it for you?' He tried to correct his grandfather. 'It's called a watch, Grandpa Joe, not a knife. You got it wrong.' The old man threw a tantrum. He remembered feeling distressed and scared; he had asked his father what was wrong with Grandpa Joe. The grandfather he had known and loved had ceased to be.

* * *

Kadek didn't bring him to the clinic in Denpasar. Instead, they went to the gleaming white, brand new hospital near Kuta, which was custom-made for tourists and expats on the island. It was one of the things he disliked about being a traveller who didn't know the local language. He disliked the self-enforced segregation that perpetuated this separate existence: between those from the outside world and those from the island. Between those who had money and those who didn't. Between those who could speak the language and those who didn't. In his eyes, it was unnatural.

His doctor was a tall, tanned Aussie who was probably a few years younger than he. It was easy enough for him to prescribe medication (topical and oral) for the rashes but the memory lapses were more difficult to treat. It was hard for him to explain to the doctor; after all it was very subjective. And they would have to get into his medical history and state of mind, at least for

the past year or two to have a basis for comparison. At the end of the consultation, the doctor just intoned that it sounded like 'mild memory impairment, probably due to stress' and was, in all probability, not serious. He said it was most likely temporary, and at this moment, didn't justify an MRI to see if there was a real problem. The doctor told him that he probably needed to learn some relaxation techniques and perhaps try some mineral supplements.

He was silent on the way home. It would take over an hour on this small highway they called Bypass Ngurah Rai. Kadek sensed his disquiet and he switched on the car stereo. He played a CD with all those sad, quavering Balinese ballads; he had the volume turned up high.

He kept asking himself what would justify the MRI? If he suffered a complete loss of memory? If he forgot to take his bath for a week? Or started walking around town in his bathrobe or worse, naked, with no idea of where and who he was? He just prayed it would never get to that. He'd rather slit his wrists than endure the indignity of losing his mind. Losing his words. But if he ever got to that, he wouldn't be aware of too much, really. He imagined it would be like being lost in a strange and bewildering country; lost in a territory with no signposts, no guidebooks, no one to show you the way.

*　*　*

It had been a month since the visit to the doctor and it seemed like not a day would past without Kadek appearing with some local remedy for healing the mind and the soul. There were

strange herbs which had to be boiled. Roots and herbs wrapped in banana leaves and recycled bottles filled with vile-looking and pungent potions would be left on his doorstep. These covert deliveries would be accompanied by late night calls from Kadek with convoluted instructions on how to prepare them. For his part, he would take all of these concoctions inside his kitchen and after trying out two of the potions out of courtesy, he immediately disposed of the rest as soon as he received them. Kadek was a gentle, kind-hearted soul, and this was his way of saying that he cared and that he would do all that he could to help him get through this. And then of course, there were the shamans.

Kadek had insisted that on the western part of the island there was a shaman who was a powerful healer. He could rid sufferers of any black magic hexes and mysterious illnesses. Because of his island-wide reputation, there were many others seeking his ministrations so they would have to be at the shaman's house very early in the morning and wait for their turn. In any case it would be an interesting departure from his routine at home. And what if the session did succeed in helping him with his memory problems? He had nothing to lose and everything to gain.

It was seven o'clock in the morning when they arrived at the healer's home. They had been on the road for one and a half hours. It had been raining heavily all the way to the house. Some of the ditches were overflowing, turning the narrow village roads into temporary streams of rushing, loamy water. They had to park almost half a kilometre away as there were many cars already there. They ran to the house using a flimsy, broken umbrella that buckled under the strong gusts of wind. When they got inside, there were people waiting on the sodden veranda. Some of them

were too sick to care if they got wet. Their families shielded them with blankets, or whatever they could get their hands on: pieces of plastic or soggy newspapers. One emaciated, half-naked young man, clad only in a damp sarong, shivered in the corner.

When it was his turn, he sat in front of the healer as the man covered him with pungent smoke from the incense. Then the healer sprinkled holy water on him as he chanted a mantra. His eyes were stinging from the smoke. He had to keep them shut for a moment; tears were welling in them. He was overcome with emotion. 'What am I doing in this place? Why on earth did I allow Kadek to bring me here?' He felt an overwhelming sense of loss, as if he had ceded all logic, all control by being there. All he wanted to do was to get out at once and head home. The safest place in the world was always in front of his laptop, writing. The words would keep him sane; the words would restore order in his life.

*　*　*

In a storybook world, the visit to the healer would have done the trick. He would have been miraculously cured and his mind would function better than ever. But there was no change in his condition. Kadek said that it was probably because he didn't have enough faith in the healer's efficacy. He said faith was the key; otherwise the Gods wouldn't bestow their favour. He nodded in agreement. It was true. He had doubted the healer almost as much as he doubted himself. He didn't believe in miracles or magical cures. He was no longer in awe of the world and the surprises it offered. His life had been charted without his acquiescence.

He had begun to jot down everything, from the most mundane (*pay gardener on Tuesday – his name: Nyoman; mend brown pants; lock back door before sleeping*) to the more profound – all his recollections from his childhood, his parents, falling in love, his children growing up – each time these fleeting thoughts surfaced. And all the other emotions that have been appearing as he coped with his diminishing mind and aging body. He was thankful that his concerns had nothing to do with vanity. He could be accused of many other flaws but certainly, conceit had never been one of them. His biggest fear was losing his autonomy; of having to rely on someone else for his movements and to provide him with clarity of thought.

Liz, his agent, called him late one night, their inimitable way of speaking for over two decades was to dispense with conversational niceties and preamble. It was a precedent they had set from the early days when he was travelling in some remote corner of the world and he had to call her via a satellite telephone – now they were conditioned to speak to one another with an economy of words. 'So what's the matter with you?' she said in greeting. She had sensed that something was wrong from the terse e-mails they had been sending each other. And he answered by telling her everything, from his fear that he had some form of dementia, to his feelings of futility and his anxiety about the future. She listened to him without uttering a word. And when he was done she just said, 'Look, come home and we'll find the best specialists in the country to fix it. It's not a foregone conclusion.'

Foregone conclusions were something of an anathema for him. It was a foregone conclusion that he would make a fine career out of journalism. But he had left the stability of a

salaried position at a prestigious magazine to become a writer. In his father's eyes it was a precarious existence based on strong will and fancy ideas, and not much else. Not exactly a suitable vocation for a man with a young wife and two small boys. Later, it was a foregone conclusion that he would stay married (for the sake of the boys) even though his wife was adamant that she was better off with another man. With a man who didn't suffer from perpetual wanderlust; a man who was around long enough to make her happy; a man with no emotional intimacy issues. (He remembered, towards the end of their marriage, how her anger was always couched in irritating psycho-babble – thanks to all the self-help books that she stockpiled at home and the many sessions with the shrink that he had paid for grudgingly.)

It would be a foregone conclusion amongst his family and friends (if they had been privy to his condition because for now his only confidants were Liz and Kadek) that he should surrender his life as he knew it and opt for all sorts of cutting-edge medical tests and treatments back home. But that sounded too much like capitulation to him. He felt strongly that the best option for him was to stay on in Bali and write. He would try to finish his book on Mongolia and then he would leave the island forever. After all, there was so much more of the world to be seen. He needed to experience again the mystery of other places and other people as they unfold for the first time. Perhaps that would give him a more measured perspective of his situation. And perhaps it might buy him more time for memories. Memories that he sorely needed: both the old, and the making of the new.

THE FEUD

Eliza abhorred conflict. Especially loud and ugly confrontations. It wasn't due to any cowardice on her part but merely that she hated the emotional involvement it required. She preferred being pleasantly detached from the nastiness and pettiness of human interaction. She was blissfully happy in her simple home, surrounded by her books and her six cats (if they weren't being gobbled up by the resident pythons). Twice a week Ketut Astri, a lovely girl from the village nearby, would come in and help her clean the place. Once a week she would venture out of her safe haven to get some groceries, go to the post office and check out the bookstore. Every few months she would either go trekking or bird-watching.

When she first started her working life, she had fancied herself as something of a writer – this after toiling for many years as an editor at a newspaper. She had seen enough of bad writing to know that she had a knack of stringing words together to come up with good, neat prose. After all, words were something she could control and arrange at will. (Human beings, though, with their wilfulness and foibles were a different matter altogether.) She had submitted several pieces to various magazines (under pseudonyms, of course) and they were all published.

At one time she thought she could make a go of it as a travel

writer, jetting off to all sorts of exotic places on someone else's tab, writing about it and getting paid handsomely. Not a bad arrangement she thought. So she tried it a few times but she quickly grew weary of the life. It soon became obvious that she really had to engage with the local populace to discover a place. It wasn't enough to go traipsing off alone, exploring the sights, reading various guidebooks and surmising what it was like to live there. She had to interact with people at length and understand how they lived. It was too taxing.

For one there were lecherous men who seemed to think a woman travelling alone was an automatic invitation for a casual dalliance. Everything revolved around sex with these men. The popular line was: 'You must be lonely without male company'. And then there were those who deemed any person from her country 'wealthy' and thereby obliged to fork out money for every unfortunate expense they had to bear for their family. ('I don't have enough money for my son's school fees.' Or: 'My mother is very, very sick.') She was always very torn between wanting to help and wanting to escape. When she gave, she always felt duped, and when she didn't part with her money, she always felt like a selfish, materialistic boor.

So travel writing didn't agree with her and she tried her hand at romance writing. A publisher friend told her there was good money to be made in churning out stories about torrid love affairs that ended happily ever after. That, she discovered, required an even greater stretch of imagination for her because quite frankly she didn't understand what was all the fuss about love. She had had a few boyfriends in her day but she always stumbled on the question of intimacy. The men always wanted more than she was

able to provide. They demanded protestations of undying love, which always seemed farcical to her. And insofar as the physical expressions of love, well, those always made her feel awkward and exposed. She could think of a dozen things she'd rather do than to have sex.

So the romance writing fizzled out just like her past passions. But she had always been thrifty and smart about her money. Right after she started her first job, she had invested in a retirement plan. At thirty-nine, she cashed out with a handsome sum of money with which to live comfortably and travel a fair bit. She found herself in Bali by pure coincidence. She was supposed to fly to Hong Kong to meet an internet beau. He sounded intelligent and intriguing but she had a nagging feeling he was much better in the virtual world than in person. But as fate would have it there was a typhoon and no flights could get to Hong Kong, so she opted to go to Bali instead. It was sheer providence. She loved it enough to make a down payment on a small house and within two months she had packed up her life back home and started a new one in Pundian.

Her new home was located in a verdant river gorge. It had belonged to a Dutchman who had returned to Europe to die. There was a steep driveway leading down from the main road to her compound. The house comprised of three tiny buildings: kitchen, bedroom with an adjoining open-air bathroom and living room. It was spartan but charming. She had a wide uninterrupted view of the entire ravine where she was the only human inhabitant. She spent her days reading, writing her journals, cooking and tending to her cats. She had even started a garden, with one section for local medicinal herbs. Ketut and her brother helped her with

that. Her home was the kind of place one could grow old in quiet contentment. It was everything she had dreamt of.

Then the villa developers appeared. For months they ravaged the hill slope on the opposite side of the gorge from her; felling the beautiful tall, old trees without a care and dredging up huge quantities of soil that muddied the river below. After all the carnage, they came up with five ultra-modern luxury villas and a sleek clubhouse with a gleaming swimming pool. From the first night they had their official villa launch party, Eliza never again experienced the calm and tranquillity that she had enjoyed for four glorious years. The longest silence she had after the arrival of the villa people was perhaps a week and then it would resume: music blaring from incessant parties, hoots and cackles of laughter reverberating through the ravine, or clamorous conversations starting in the day and extending long into the wee hours of the night.

One day, right after she had taken a long shower alfresco in her Bali-style open bathroom, she noticed flashes of light from the direction of the clubhouse. She used the binoculars from her bird-watching expeditions and her worst fears were confirmed. They had installed a telescope in the clubhouse and it was trained right on her bathroom! She was incensed. She could feel the blood rushing to her head. She considered the many violent ways she would seek revenge. She just couldn't believe the audacity of the villa owners. What barbarians! No wonder their villa guests were ill-mannered louts. They were entirely of the same repulsive ilk.

But because she hated face-to-face confrontation there was no way she would stoop to talking with those pigs. Finally after deciding against lobbing a Molotov cocktail into the clubhouse

she thought of an ideal way to get even. At first she was only going to place one, right in front of her bathroom; to defend her modesty and also to express her extreme displeasure. The mirror was big and round, almost three feet in diameter and it had a wonderful way of reflecting and focussing the sun's rays onto any offending party in its path. But she ended up placing a few more in strategic positions so that the poolside and each villa would have their fair share of the blinding light from her 'mirrors of retribution', as she liked to think of them.

One day she found a note on her front gate. The message was clear. 'You stupid bitch, get rid of the fucking mirrors or we'll have to get rid of you.' She was startled by the language and the threat but she refused to be intimidated. The very next day she went to the village and spoke to the owner of the land around her. She leased as many acres of land as she could from him (with the first option to buy) and she bought more mirrors. If they wanted a war, they would get one. For the first time in a long time she slept like a baby.

But the vicious thugs reciprocated by scratching her car and killing two of her cats with poisoned meat. Her fury knew no bounds. It called for guerrilla tactics. Any of her actions would be righteous because they had crossed the line when they murdered poor innocent Fluffy and Ginger. Cold-blooded killers they were. They would have to pay. And pay dearly they would in more ways than one. In any case there was no way she would be chased from her own home without a good fight. But first she needed to buy a strong net and to enlist the help of Ketut's brother, Nyoman. (Although for his own good, she couldn't tell him what she was really up to.)

THE OTHER SIDE

Timothy considered himself to be an easy-going guy. He liked a good laugh now and then: a rollicking good party, a good booze-up with a bunch of friends and a good time with the ladies but most of all he loved making good money. He was once an investment banker but the burn-out came early. Fortunately for him he had already made a handsome sum from the stock market. He quickly invested these in some mutual funds and property in various countries across the globe. At forty-three, he had no financial worries. No worries of any kind. Until he started his first development in Bali, that is.

The small villa development was in effect a pilot project. The first in a series of building projects all around the island. He had bought enough property all around the world to learn a thing a two about what made a building a good one: from its location, architectural design, building material, landscaping, property management and maintenance. He wanted to have more control over every aspect of his property investments and there was no better way of doing that than getting into the business himself. It was a challenge learning a new trade but he had been getting bored with his semi-retirement. He had been coasting along when what he really needed was a project to keep the adrenalin pumping.

Three years ago he had bought a six-bedroom house in a gated compound in Sanur. The place was really a magnificent showpiece. The well-manicured Balinese style garden was the envy of many. The huge swimming pool and jacuzzi made it an ideal place for barbecues and parties. So far his best friend from home and a cousin had had their wedding receptions at the house.

But the house was too big for a man living alone. He thrived on company but the problem with inviting friends over was that there was no easy way to get rid of them when they had overstayed their welcome. And that was when he decided to rent a small studio villa in Seminyak. The space was too small for parties or stay-overs unless of course it was an assignation with one of his off and on lovers. It was the ideal residence from which to plan projects and maintain privacy when he needed it.

It also meant easy access (and egress) for his friend and partner Sam who lived nearby whenever they had to work together. This was really the main reason why he leased the villa in Seminyak. Hosting Sam at his Sanur home had begun to take its toll. Sam was a hard-working and hard-drinking man who had made his money in Bali from exporting furniture and apparel back to Europe. He had been living in Bali for fifteen years and he knew almost everyone there was to know on the island, from the local chieftains and high priests to government officials. He was proud of his working class roots and even prouder of the fact that he had accumulated his wealth without any help from anyone. He was married to a beautiful Balinese girl and although he doted on their three-year-old son, he was fast getting bored with his young wife. And so he found every opportunity he could to bring his other love interests and lusty discoveries of the week to Timothy's Sanur residence.

At first Timothy didn't mind Sam's illicit trysts in his home. After all what were friends for? But then Ika, Sam's wife, started calling him, tearfully asking for Sam's whereabouts. The first few times it was easy enough to provide various alibis that centred on business or fictitious trips around the island in search of land for

their proposed villa projects. Most of these excuses were after all grounded in some truth. But Sam's extra-marital activities became more frequent and more rowdy. Timothy could hardly sleep a wink when in their throes of passion, Sam and his girls groaned, moaned, shrieked and rocked the house down, all through the night. Sleep deprivation was one thing but then Ika started appearing at the front gate, carrying their little boy, Wayan Sam Junior, crying and ranting about her misbehaving husband. He was forced to put a stop to all the nonsense and he did. He rented the studio villa in Seminyak and locked up his Sanur house.

Sam and he always joked that they had a regular 'Good Cop, Bad Cop' routine to clinch their business negotiations. His role was always the even-tempered and courteous one while Sam was the uncouth and abrasive partner who demanded the lowest prices and the best terms for anything they wanted to purchase. It seemed to work well enough; allowing them to get the deal they wanted after Timothy had diplomatically smoothed any ruffled feathers with soothing words and his gentle demeanour. If only they knew how cold and calculative he really was when it came to making money. And if anyone looked long enough they would know that Sam was actually the kind-hearted and generous one despite his quick temper and generous use of profanity.

Everything had gone well with the first development in Pundian. They had found an ideal location in a quiet river gorge to build their five-villa compound. The layout of the project was an architectural feat – he had worked closely with a talented Balinese artist for the design. They used the best construction material they could find in Bali and they imported whatever else they needed from Thailand and Malaysia. Money was no object,

because this pilot project was meant to be a showcase to lure potential investors and tenants.

Sam was tireless in overseeing the day-to-day operations at the project site. Timothy was just concerned that his haranguing presence amongst the architect and his workmen would be more of a detriment than a help. But Sam insisted, after all he had poured good money into the villas and he had a vested interest to make sure everything proceeded perfectly. And it did. Timothy didn't have any major doubts to the contrary; after all he was not the kind of businessman whom left anything to chance. With Sam's help, he had hand-picked the most skilled and suitable people in Bali for the job.

The only real glitch was the weather. Three consecutive days of rain meant there was some work stoppage but of course he had already included such delays into the contingency allocation. The completion date was only off by five days but in the end it was worth the wait. The villas were really quite marvellous to behold, stunning with its bold combination of glass, concrete, polished wood panels and metal cladding. It was a pleasure to relax at one of the villa's patios or at the poolside, surrounded by the lush jungle. Beneath the sounds of the birds and cicadas, the roar of the river could be heard rushing through the bottom of the gorge.

With Sam's gung-ho marketing and the support from a leading property manager in Bali and Singapore, they had managed to book the villas solid for almost six years in advance. The only stipulation for any guests was that they had to enjoy plenty of music and merriment. Loud parties were after all a way of life at Villa Ria Rimba, where a DJ would be on call till the wee hours

of the morning at the music console and Sam at the well-stocked bar in the clubhouse.

Trouble started when Sam and a young male guest noticed the blonde woman living alone on the other side of the gorge. They were consumed with curiosity about her; an interest which had emerged during the quiet moments of the day when the others were nursing their hangovers and resting from their wild antics of the previous night. Then crazy Sam came back with a high-powered telescope, which he set up at one of the clubhouse windows, giving him an unfettered view of the woman as she moved around her house, eating and cooking, doing her gardening, working on her computer, feeding her numerous cats. And then one day he was delirious with joy: he started yelling for all the men to come to the telescope and take a closer look at the woman as she was taking a shower in her outdoor bathroom. The woman did have a nice body even though there was no doubt that she was no longer a sweet young thing. She had firm breasts and lovely buttocks. No cellulite in sight. In fact she looked a damned sight better naked than with her clothes on. Sam began to spend more and more time at the telescope with the ardent hope of more intimate glimpses of his bathing Venus.

It kept him out of mischief for a time, but even that didn't last long. Somehow the woman discovered that she was being watched and she started to put up the first of those blasted mirrors. It was downright uncomfortable for anyone wanting to laze around on their patio or at the poolside during the day. Those blinding rays made it unpleasant even for anyone just standing outside, wanting to look at the jungle. And then she put up more. Sam of course retaliated in the most foolhardy way. Instead of reasoning with

the woman, he wrote a nasty note. And that was when the mirrors started mushrooming.

Of course Sam went berserk. He came back one day muttering something about keying the woman's car and making a couple of her cats real sick just to ram the message home. The bitch was nuts, he kept insisting. Timothy didn't agree with such strong-arm tactics but Sam was beyond persuasion. The feud with this woman had become personal; he had taken it as an affront to his manhood. And he wanted to make bloody sure that she would leave the gorge, crying and snivelling like a frightened child. Just as Sam planned his next attack, the guests started complaining that there was an overpowering stench emanating from beneath the villas, possibly from somewhere right underneath the patio. They looked everywhere they could think of but they still couldn't find the source of the foul smell. And right about then, the blonde girl who was staying at Villa No. 5 came out of her bathroom screaming like a banshee, with her panties and shorts around her ankles.

When she was done with her hysterical howling, she tearfully explained that she was sitting on the toilet bowl 'doing her number two' and reading a magazine when she saw a huge snake on the floor, right next to the wall behind the toilet bowl. She ran out of there as fast as she could. About twenty minutes after that another snake was found by the couple in Villa No. 1 just as they were having sex in the sunken bath-tub. That snake was hiding on the towel rack, cosily nestled between the folded bath towels. They said the snake appeared to be looking at them as they were going at it. But there were more than just the two pythons, another two were found. One was underneath a poolside deckchair while

another was curled behind the whiskey bottles in the bar.

Guests from three villas insisted on a refund, they had packed all their belongings and they said they wanted to move to another hotel as soon as possible. Sam was livid. He almost got into a brawl with one of the guests after calling the man a 'gutless sissy'. Timothy just looked on in disbelief. It was time for him to step in. Sam was out of control. This feud had brought out the worst in him and it was obvious he didn't possess the necessary acumen to run the villas. Timothy packed Sam and everyone else off that very night. Some would stay at his house in Sanur while others would be put up at another resort in the area. Villa Ria Rimba would have to be vacated until the situation could be resolved.

Tomorrow he would visit his neighbour across the gorge. Perhaps before that he would look for a kitten, or maybe two, as peace offering. In the meantime all he could do was to try to get some sleep and pray that he survived the night.

SUNSET

The sun was shining bright, a brilliant eye-watering orb, hovering above the horizon like a celestial disco-ball. The sky was a vast expanse of cobalt blue, the colour of his mother's irises in spring, overlaid with some flourishes of wispy cotton-candy clouds. There were hardly any waves. There weren't any people or boats nearby. The water was at the level of his chest but he was now getting steadily deeper with each step and he started treading it at a relaxed pace. The sea was warm and comforting – he felt buoyant and supported – this was probably how it was like thirty-six years ago in his mother's womb. He felt the warmth spread through his body and his senses dulling from the alcohol and the anti-histamine pills. He felt good and infallible and all-knowing.

In about half an hour the sun would almost be touching the horizon and then it would drift below it, sinking out of sight. He wanted to swim towards the sun as it descended. His plan was to reach it, to become one with the light as it disappeared from the lowest limits of the sky. His body was beginning to feel heavier but he now believed that he could do anything he put his mind to. Nothing was insurmountable. All was possible. The sun with its shimmering golden-copper trail on the water would be his guide.

* * *

It was a year and eight months ago that he had arrived in Bali full of hope and with exactly 12,000 dollars to his name. The plan was that he would rent a small place, live very frugally and start his small business developing websites for other expats in Bali as well as for other businesses farther afield. His friend Tim said that he made a good living with his online business, and that the cost of living was cheap and that the dollar could stretch a lot farther than back home. Judging by the photos of the beautiful villa he now had, and the beautiful Balinese woman who lived with him, Tim had made quite a success of his life in Bali. And he wanted that.

Between the freezing winters and the dead-end jobs that he floated in and out of, anywhere beyond the county limits was welcomed. Tim, his good friend since high school, another geek just like him, had travelled to Bali with his mother and sister but he decided that he preferred to stay rather than to go back to his dreary job and his life in the renovated basement of his family house.

His own life was not much different to Tim's. He still lived in the old house he grew up in but his bedroom was behind the kitchen. This was the room his parents lived in in the last few years of their lives when they could no longer manage the stairs. The three bedrooms upstairs had become his sister Terry's domain, now that she was married and planning a new family. Her husband, Randy, a tall, burly guy with ginger hair, had moved in with a huge assortment of gear for hunting and fishing as well as a large collection of clothes for his outdoor escapades. Randy was in law enforcement: he was an under-sheriff in their town. He got very tongue-tied when he was around Randy. Randy tried

hard to engage him in light conversation and some convivial male bonding but he felt even more inept, inarticulate and awkward. They had nothing in common except for a brief stint in the church choir when they were both in grade school.

It wasn't too long before he stopped using the front door altogether for fear of running into Randy. He couldn't bear having another beer with him while pretending to be interested in the football or baseball game blaring on the TV when all he wanted was to get to his room and onto his computer. He couldn't bear having to act as if he was comfortable in his own home with the oversized interloper who was trying hard to be kind to him. He couldn't bear trying to think of a good subject to talk about in their stilted conversations. He stealthily walked around the house to the back door, entering into the kitchen silently and straight into his bedroom. It was not long before he planned his movements to avoid Randy and his sister completely. Their limited interaction amounted to quick reminders hollered through his closed bedroom door in the mornings or hastily written messages left on the old family refrigerator, pinned under the neon pink fridge magnet of two pigs kissing – a relic from a family outing to the county fair many years ago.

* * *

He had always felt small back home. It was a constant embarrassment that he had to shop in the children's section of JC Penney. He often had to reconnoitre the store first to make sure that there was no one there whom he knew. He was so fed-up of making up clumsy lies about how he was shopping for a

non-existent younger cousin who lived out of state. He would explain his selections with his face reddening by the minute, his body rebelling against the fib he was expressing. When that person had moved to another part of the store, he would rush to the cashier – with his face, ears and neck now a beetroot-red – to pay for the two football jerseys (in the size for boys' ages thirteen to fourteen), a pair of jeans as well as three boxer shorts and undershirts.

So it was with the greatest happiness that he found himself on an island where he was of average size, heck, sometimes he was even taller than some of the locals. He felt like the long lost son who was finally returned to his tribe. And this simple fact made him grin inside and out. The Balinese were always polite and although the men's fondness for touching his hand or slipping a friendly arm around his shoulder left him quite alarmed at first, he soon found out that there was nothing 'gay' about such physical displays of amity. It was culturally just the way Balinese people interacted with one another. And the girls were unlike any women that he had ever met. They were gentle and yet poised, smiling and talking to him like he mattered. They would look directly into his eyes to engage him in conversation in their broken English and it made him feel like a teenager again. They didn't seem to judge him one way or another. He wanted to impress them but he had no idea how to communicate without coming on strong like a typical horny foreigner wanting to get into their pants.

He bought a basic two-stroke motorbike and rented a small house in a quiet local neighbourhood by paying in advance for two years. He was one of two foreigners who lived there. The other was a middle-aged German lady who was married to a

Balinese man. His home was just an eight-minute ride to the hub of the community where transplants from Europe, Australia, North and South America had set up a vibrant community of chic boutiques, surfer hangouts and cafés. Once he overheard a fellow American loudly lament that the place was no different from any of the colonised spaces in Goa, Phuket or Tamarindo. Since he had never been to any of those places, he didn't understand why the guy complained that it was a 'soulless tourist enclave'.

He tried hard to make new friends with the other foreigners in the community but since he didn't surf, or do yoga or own a business like most of them did, he quickly ran out of conversation. He did forge a friendship of sorts with his landlady's son, Wayan. Wayan tried to introduce him to his other friends. And so he was persuaded to join their convoy of about eight motorbikes to ride around to the far side of the island and back just to eat fish satay in Goa Lawah, or to watch a movie or hang out at the air-conditioned shopping malls in Kuta. As much as he appreciated the company he was beginning to have the old familiar sense of discomfiture, of being out of place and out of synch. Perhaps the truth was the boys were much too young for him to be with and the expense was beginning to weigh on him as he always felt obliged to pay for all their outings because he was the oldest. And being the sole foreigner, it was taken for granted that he was also the one with the most money to spare.

He soon decided that it was high time he put serious time and effort into starting up his website designing company. He had come over to Bali with two new clients from the US who wanted websites for their small businesses, and so he was quite relieved to be able to seek refuge in the comfort of his programming codes

and the comforting anonymity of the internet. As it was too hot for him to work in his room during the day he settled into the routine of working at a café nearby. The place was quite empty during the day except for the odd tourists who would come in sweaty and tired after sightseeing and shopping in the area. He didn't really speak to anyone but after two weeks of coming in like clockwork around half past ten in the morning and leaving around half past eight at night, the wait staff soon got to know his name and what he liked to order. Although he knew having all his meals at a café meant for tourists and expats was a big daily expense, he couldn't imagine going anywhere else to spend the day.

Most of the time he was so engrossed in his work that he hardly noticed what was going on around him. He knew that people would come in, have a meal or a drink, and then leave. He rarely made eye contact with the other customers. It was easier that way. He didn't have to make small talk and he didn't have to answer uncomfortable questions. And at this point of his adjustment to Bali, most questions from tourists, especially the ones from his own country, made him squirm. He always felt as if he had to justify his existence on the island. And so he kept his headphones on and kept his gaze fixed on the screen of his laptop.

When his eyes got tired, he would stare outside to the patchy green soccer field where a motley crew of stray dogs and local kids would be running around playing catch or soccer. He sometimes wished he could just let off steam and join them but it was obvious that it would be awkward. At times he would try to catch the eye of the serving staff, where in hushed tones he would order a hot Americano or a Coke, always with no ice. He knew he was

drinking way too much soda for his own good but the cans were always icy cold and it offered a vague connection to his old life where his old fridge back home was always stocked with several six-packs of Coca-Cola.

He almost always ordered a burger for his meal. Sometimes it would be a basic pasta dish. Once he thought he would be adventurous and he ordered a *nasi goreng spesial*. The fried rice was deliriously spicy with its combination of unknown condiments and herbs, topped with a fried egg. The dish was so strange that he felt as if his guts were on fire. He kept belching after that meal and each searing belch brought up an aftertaste of garlic and coriander, propelled by the gassy pressure of the Coke. He had to rush back to his rented house and take a big swig of his precious Pepto-Bismol – the one and only bottle brought from home – before he could stand up straight again.

* * *

After learning his lesson, he steered clear from any of the spicy local dishes and kept to a steady diet of mild meatball and spaghetti, hamburgers, and scrambled eggs with toast. The wait staff seemed to know his preferred menu choices, which didn't vary too much from day to day. They didn't try to engage him in conversation because he always seemed to be busy at his laptop even when they were at his table to serve his food and drink orders. That is until one day when Dayu came along. She had put his food down on the empty side of the table, but she just stood there looking at him until he just couldn't ignore her.

'Mr Mike, why you never eat local food? You don't like?' she

asked him with a look of genuine interest.

'Well, I have tried to eat it a few times but I can't handle it,' he replied, his cheeks burning at the attention; he wondered if any of the other guests were listening.

'Can't handle?'

'My stomach is not used to the spiciness. It's much too hot for me. I get sick.' He rubbed his abdomen vigorously to explain.

'Oh. How pity you. I think why Mr Mike eat same food all the time. Very boring.'

'No, no, not boring. Just safer.'

'More safer and more boring. Next time you drink mango *lassi*. Koki, er … chef … make good mango *lassi*. Good for stomach. You try, okay? I give you one glass. Free for you.'

And with those kind words from Dayu, he was inexorably hooked. She wasn't particularly beautiful but she was gentle and always smiling with her beautiful white, straight teeth, full lips, high forehead and curly black hair which she always kept neatly in a bun with a small frangipani tucked into it. And she always appeared concerned about his well-being: asking him what he had eaten that day and why he was working so hard all the time and how was his stomach, his health, his family back home.

He began looking out for her every day, trying to find out as casually as he could from the others when was her shift for the week. Most days, he could see her come into work on her motorbike. He had never seen any man sending her to the café so this was a promising sign. She was probably still single and this thought made him feel happy. On the days when she was not around he would be so distracted and his productivity slipped right away. He just couldn't think and he would end up surfing

the net or Skype-ing (even though the café didn't allow it) with some friends back home. He would get restless and despondent and he would end his day much earlier than usual; often ending up at home, in front of the TV, watching an action DVD where the plot was a noisy blur of explosions, car chases and plenty of gratuitous violence.

He would later find out from Dayu that there was a big religious ceremony or *upacara* at her village and she had to help her family out with the preparations because her father was overseeing some of the religious ceremonies. It all sounded important and exotic to him but Dayu didn't make it sound grand or impressive. It was just life as usual in the village and as much as she was proud of her village and her culture, she always looked weary and sleepy when she returned from these extended absences for an *upacara*. Her other life in the village made her seem mysterious and even more separate from him. It made her all the more desirable.

He started to ask her all sorts of question about her village. About her family, her many siblings, particularly about her father, the patriarch of the entire village. Her father was a well-respected healer and an artist. But his increased responsibilities at the village temple meant that he did less of his art. She proudly showed him photographs of her father's many intricate drawings of Bali mythology done in black ink, of beautiful goddesses, one astride a swan, another standing in a huge lotus blossom; while other paintings were of the Bali landscape; with vibrant depictions of traditional life painted in acrylic. There was one of the village market, at harvest time in the rice fields, at a cockfight, a cremation ceremony, and all painted in such great detail that every available space on the canvas had a story to tell. He was

mesmerised.

He asked her for photographs of the village, the ceremonies, her family and she obliged. When the café was quiet, she would bashfully bring her mobile phone or her small digital camera over to his table to show him photos of her family and her home. The colourful photographs of smiling family members in their best ceremonial outfits of lace, gold brocades, rich batiks; of sombre priests clad in all white; and of sacred, ancient rites; all emphasised the fact that they came from two very different worlds.

What on earth could a boy from the American Mid-West have in common with a girl from a small village at the foot of a volcanic mountain in Bali? This thought kept him awake at nights but there was no denying the fact that he wanted Dayu more than ever after learning and seeing more of her family and home through the photos. He knew that he wanted to ask her out on a date but he was worried that making such an overture would damage their budding friendship. And so he restrained himself even as he became more and more infatuated with her.

* * *

As fate would have it, it was Dayu who changed the course of their budding friendship. They were friendly enough now that she dropped the Mister before his name. He cherished the very few times she called him by his name, but it was as if this nascent intimacy made her shy and hesitant and so she tried her best not to have to call him Mike at all.

'I want to invite you to my village. For ceremony. We call *melaspas*.'

'Me-las-pas', he repeated, stressing and stretching each syllable to conceal his surprise and delight.

'Yes, *melaspas*. Special *upacara* for new building in my house. We have new *bale daja*. How you say, master room, for my father and mother. We make bigger and better, now with AC. So we must do special blessing.'

'But I don't have anything decent to wear. I don't have a sarong or that headgear.' He gesticulated towards his crown agitatedly.

'*Udeng*? Don't worry, you can borrow. We ask Ketut.' Without waiting for him to reply she went to get Ketut, another waiter at the café. They spoke for a few minutes and Ketut came to his table smiling widely.

'Mr Mike, you borrow my *adat* clothes, okay? I help you wear the *kamen* and *saput*, and the *udeng* properly. Don't worry. I bring you to Dayu's village. With me and my wife – we are going. I drive you.'

He really didn't know if he wanted to jump for joy or just hide in fear. This was it. This could be the test to see if her family could accept him. He had to do his best not to stick out like a sore thumb.

He slept fitfully as the day for the ceremony neared. He would wake up in the middle of the night, pace around the bedroom, then he would march out into the living room and then he would sit out on the patio in the dark, drinking a cold bottle of Bintang until the mosquitoes became unbearable.

He would pass the mirror in the hallway, catch a glimpse of his own reflection and he wished that he was more tanned. Why didn't he spend more time in the sun in all the months here, he chided himself. And his hair! Why couldn't it be darker, not this

light colour of straw that would surely stand out in a Balinese crowd.

*   *   *

He was quiet all the way to Dayu's village. Ketut tried to engage him in conversation but his taciturn responses made it clear that he was not in a mood for light banter. Ketut then started chatting to his wife and he was left to manage his troubling thoughts: What if her family didn't like him? What if everything was much too alien for him to accept? What if he couldn't stomach any of the food? What if they put ice in their drinks? What if it got too hot for him especially in this costume? Randy would surely laugh his balls of if he could see him now wrapped in two layers of sarong and a rolled napkin on his head.

When they arrived at the village they had to park some distance away from the house as there were many cars, motorbikes, even a few pick-up trucks parked on the side of the road. He could hear a *gamelan* band going at it full force. It wasn't an intimate family affair – this was a village event.

He stopped right in the middle of the road when he realised how big of a ceremony it was. He grabbed Ketut's arm in panic.

'What's wrong, Mr Mike?'

'Hang on a minute. I need to rest for a minute.'

'You're not well?' Ketut peered closely at his face and then cast a worried look at his wife.

'I'm … I have to catch my breath. Just give me a minute.'

'Do you want water? I Luh has water,' he said as he gestured to his wife for the bottle of Aqua.

He was just about to sit right on the road when he heard

his name and Ketut's being called out. It was Dayu. She looked beautiful in a white lace top and a yellow batik sarong. She ran towards them and he jumped up to his feet, forcing a big smile on his face.

Ketut said something to her in Balinese and she looked worried.

'You feel sick? You need to lie down?'

He waved her off telling her it was nothing, just the heat and humidity. But she was already at his side, holding onto his forearm, leading him into her compound.

They were all brought to a small brick building with a large raised veranda, covered in beautiful green tiles. There was an ornately carved and gilded Balinese door, kept closed, which led to a small, narrow room. Up some steps onto the veranda there was a woven rattan mat laid out with trays of Thermos and jugs filled with hot and cold drinks and an assortment of colourful gelatinous and creamy sweets, in bright pink, green, beige, yellow. There was a dignified older man in all white and plenty of gold jewellery and a deferential younger man next to him, smoking and chatting quietly in the midst of the bustle of people coming and going from the other side of the compound. Overhead there was a ceiling fan going full blast. He was glad to be able to sit in silence for a moment. Ketut had joked the veranda was the VIP section. Dayu had left him alone there to take Ketut and I Luh to where all the other guests had congregated. Various people stopped to greet the older man with more respect than the Balinese normally displayed and then they were off to the back. Perhaps Ketut wasn't joking about this being the VIP section after all.

Moments later Dayu was back to check in on him, she had

brought him a plate piled with white rice and crispy barbequed meat and a vegetable slaw of greens, beansprouts and coconut flakes. Eat, eat, she commanded him. She poured him a glass of a bright pink cordial with ice cubes in it and she must have seen the alarmed look he gave the ice. 'Oh okay, you don't like ice in Bali. Here, a bottle of Aqua for you.' And then she was gone again. No time to chat, no time for him to get to know the family. He started eating the food slowly and to his surprise it was all very tasty. The meat wasn't too spicy but the vegetables harboured some potent bits of chillies in it. Still it tasted good so he ate all the vegetables covered by heaped spoonsful of rice to lessen the burn.

When he was done eating and without standing up, he shuffled his bottom to a wall by the ornate door so that he could lean against it. His legs were stretched out straight because he just couldn't cross them the way the locals could. The older man and his younger friend were still deep in conversation and they were now downing glasses of black coffee and smoking the pungent clove cigarettes. They had briefly tried to engage him in conversation but there was not much they could talk about, so they went back to their own animated discussion. His stomach now full and lulled by the fan above him and the steady drone of conversation of the two, and the all-pervasive smell of cloves, his eyelids became heavier and heavier.

* * *

Earthquake was his first lucid thought. His felt his body being jostled back and forth and he opened his eyes to Ketut who was trying to wake him up. He had fallen fast asleep and he was now

lying in a foetal position in the corner. He tried to sit up but he felt as if he was beneath a heavy pile of rocks; his body was still asleep. Ketut wasn't alone – with him were his wife, Dayu and a handsome older gentleman, who turned out to be Dayu's father. They were all wide-eyed with concern. They had all thought that he had passed out, unconscious from an illness. He was mortified. This was not the first impression he wanted to make on Dayu's father.

They looked relieved and amused when they were certain that he had been fast asleep earlier and that he was well. But he was too embarrassed. He didn't even greet Dayu's father properly as he knew he should have. He slid right off the veranda, jumping onto the ground with a thud. He looked at Dayu and her father, he said thank you to them for their hospitality, and that he had to leave right away because he had work to do at home. And with that pronouncement, he marched straight out of the compound, clutching his loosened sarongs with one arm so that they wouldn't fall off right around his ankles as he hurried out. He could hear Ketut and I Luh calling out after him and chasing him as he rushed to get to Ketut's car. He turned back and he could see Ketut holding up his leather sandals. He had stomped out barefoot in his great haste to leave.

* * *

Four months would go by before he stepped back into the café. Many things had changed there. Dayu no longer worked there and the Balinese owner, Pak Agung, had hired a manager to run the place. She was a tiny, trim Australian woman of sixty who

fastidiously re-vamped the menu and watched over the restaurant staff closely. He noticed that there was less chit-chat amongst the staff and everybody was punctual for their shift.

He asked Ketut where Dayu now worked but he just shook his head, smiling. That made him even more agitated. What was that supposed to mean? Did she get a better job somewhere or was she forced to stay home in the village to help her family? All the various painful permutations played out in his head especially when he was alone at home and he sometimes thought he would lose his mind; he missed her presence at the café, he missed her concern, and her ever-present smile. So one day when he saw Ketut walking into the café at the start of his shift, he waylaid him by the side of the small stall that sold Balinese rice and dishes to the locals.

'Ketut! So where is Dayu? What happened to her?'

'Mr Mike, why you so worry? Dayu is okay. She is okay, very happy. She is in Amsterdam. She is married.'

'Married? To a Balinese guy in Amsterdam? I don't understand.'

'No, no. To a Dutch man. Hans. Her long-time boyfriend. Before he lived here many years, then he go back to work. But they write email, phone each other every day.'

He felt as if his knees were giving up on him. He had to sit down right there on the side of the pavement; he had to try to make sense of the news. A Dutch guy. But she came from the village. Her father was a high-caste healer. It wasn't possible. She would have told him about a Dutch guy. But then again, why should she have told him?

He tried hard to immerse himself in his work for the rest of

the day. Business was very slow and he had to do his best to keep his existing clients; there were three of them but really only one was worth the hours he put in. He hadn't had any income for the last two months. He had gone through all his advance and progress payments quickly. He was expecting one more payment and that was it.

He had recently spent a substantial amount of money on a 3D Blu-Ray home theatre system that was far too powerful for his small house. His new TV covered most of the wall of his living room. The speakers made the room reverberate. He spent hours watching his bootleg action DVDs. But lately he was more likely to fall asleep right in the middle of a thrilling action sequence; no amount of explosions or exciting car chases could keep him awake. And if he was being honest with himself he knew exactly why. He was just drinking far too much lately. He knew he had to cut back or go teetotal. And God only knows how much money he had spent on getting drunk, what with the sky-high prices of booze in Bali.

So he told himself that he would sit at his favourite corner table at the café until it was four o'clock and then he would go home and take a nice long nap. Then he would have dinner and maybe he'd call home to find out what his sister Terry and her husband Randy were up to these days. She'd be at home because she was due to give birth soon. Randy might be home too if he was still on the evening shift. The ultrasound had revealed that they were going to have a baby boy. He was about to be an uncle for the first time in his life and here he was thousands of miles away from home, on the other side of the world.

His sister said she wanted him to come home. 'Just pack up

everything and come home, please. You're wasting money and time there. You're not getting any younger. I want my son to know you; you're his only uncle,' she cajoled. 'Even Randy thinks it's better if you come home now. It's just not safe in those countries. It's either crazy terrorists or some weird tropical disease,' she added. 'Please come home. I really need you here, Mikey.'

His sister had never been expressive about her affection for him. At least, not so much in actual words. She used to kiss him or hug him on his birthday or at Christmas. That was it. Could she sense that he was heartbroken? Heartbroken and very soon, possibly penniless too. He wasn't about to confide in her about his life here. What could she do anyway? She and Randy would have enough on their plate with the baby coming.

* * *

After that long phone call with Terry, he told himself that he would give himself exactly three days to feel sorry for himself. He could mope, get shit-faced drunk, sleep-in, watch DVDs, eat leftovers and be a complete slob for three whole days. Then he had to clean up and face reality. He had to finish all the work he owed his clients and he had to find new work, new clients.

Or sell some of the stuff he didn't really need. Like the home theatre system. Or the ridiculously expensive dishwasher that was specially shipped in from Jakarta – when it arrived, it was such source of great amusement for the Balinese because it was such a novelty to see a machine that could actually clean dishes, pots and pans. It was unheard of not to wash your own dishes and pots

with your own hands. 'Can it scrub? No? How can you be sure everything is really clean?' They asked him, their eyes glinting with mirth. He hardly used the dishwasher. He didn't cook enough at home to require its regular use.

When the three days were up, he placed an ad in *The Bali Advertiser* with the hope that that a deep-pocketed expat or a wealthy Balinese would soon buy the dishwasher and his speakers. He needed the money as he was expected to pay for the utilities at his house and he also had to pay a Balinese agent to sort out his immigration documents, which involved circuitous dealings and numerous visits to the officials in charge.

He knew that he had to keep to his routine as much as he could so that his life – his new life without Dayu – would not be too unsettling. What was it his sister used to say, fake it till you make it? He would try to do just that now. He would feign calm and happiness until it seemed almost true.

* * *

On Tuesday morning he was back at the café. His corner table was empty as usual but after a couple of hours, the other tables filled up very quickly. The new Australian manager, Cassandra, had a new menu in place and it seemed to be a hit with the resident expats and tourists. People came to meet and eat their meals there more than the other cafés in the village. All the servers were now really busy attending to the high traffic of customers. For most of the day, he was, of course, oblivious to the brisk movement of people and food around him. He was engrossed in a particularly complicated coding when he realised that the new manager was

standing at his table.

'Michael, pardon me. I'm Cassandra, the new manager here. I'm sure Ketut and my employees have already told you about me. I want to thank you for your kind patronage of our café. They tell me that you come in almost every day and that you stay for most of the day. So yes, we're very appreciative.'

He just nodded in agreement, feeling the heat rise to his neck and face.

'Anyway, Michael, I'm sure you've noticed how busy we are now. We have a brand new menu and a wonderful new chef and people are just flocking here all through the day. So we are asking those regulars who come here to do their work or use our Wi-Fi to move upstairs.'

'Upstairs? There's an upstairs?'

'Yes, most people don't know we have a small loft upstairs that we've refurbished. The staircase is tucked away near the kitchen. The loft was used for storage and my little office but now it will have a few tables and a small TV area. You can still order food upstairs. I'm sure you will be more comfortable up there. It will be like a members' area for our regulars.'

And with that directive, he was exiled to the attic as he would refer to it in the days ahead. He was beginning to feel that no matter where he was in this world, he would always end up having to make way for other people and their grand plans. Just as it was back home, when he was told he had to move downstairs to his late parents' old bedroom so that Terry and Randy could have the entire floor upstairs.

Cassandra's decision to free up the corner table for the restaurant's increased traffic was, of course, good business

thinking but it made his life even more challenging, to say the least. The section upstairs was a snug set-up with five small tables almost back to back to one another. There were a couple of sofas and a TV for those wanting to catch a football game or the news. But the loft had limited headroom because of the thatched roof line. And of course there was the heat. Even though a small air-conditioning unit was installed in the space, the heat soared from below as the day progressed. Added with the humidity, the new area was more like a steam-room than an exclusive hangout area.

He was alone there for most of the time but there were days when a small group of men would gather to watch a soccer game. They were full of energy and they were loud, talking in a mix of languages that he thought was either French or Dutch, with a smattering of English thrown in. They ignored him completely when they were up there, so he had to resort to headphones to drown out their noise. He knew his productivity was affected by the move to the attic. Even his meals were scanty as he always had to go downstairs to put in an order, and when it finally arrived, his food was always cold. Ketut would sometimes check in on him but he had just been promoted to head server for the day shift so he was too busy.

One day the heat was almost unbearable and his spaghetti order had gone astray yet again. His usual order of ice-cold Coke in a can had arrived lukewarm. He was sweating rivulets down his face onto his laptop and his fingers kept slipping from the keyboard. He jumped up from his chair in frustration. His T-shirt was soaked with perspiration back and front. He stood up and took the T-shirt off and wiped off his body and his keyboard with

it. He hung the T-shirt on the back of his chair and he tried to resume his work. When he looked up he saw Cassandra standing at the top of the stairs staring at him with narrowed eyes.

'Michael. It looks like the heat has gotten the better of you. I know we don't have a dress code but I don't want to hear any complaints from the other customers.'

'What customers?' He pointed to the empty area.

'You know when they do come up here.'

'Cassandra, I'm almost always the only one here. And the heat up here is too damned ridiculous. My food gets here cold, if it gets here, because no servers come up here to check. I have to run downstairs all the time to place an order and then again to check on my order.'

'Well, my servers are all very busy. Perhaps you should use your mobile phone to call in your order.'

'What? What! I pay you good money for all my food and drinks. And I have been paying for quite some time. But you're not doing me any favours. No, in fact, it's the damned opposite! You treat me like shit.'

'Please mind your language, Michael.'

'I want my corner table back, Cassandra. I want you to give me back that table today. If you won't, I want to speak to the owner, now.'

'Pak Agung is much too busy to deal with your silly tantrum.'

'Now!' he shouted, taking a step closer to her.

'Michael. I warn you. There will be grave consequences.'

'What are you going to do, Cassandra? Make a citizen's arrest? I've been coming here for over a year. No issues. How long have you been working here?' he shouted.

'How dare you! I'm a respectable woman, and I run this restaurant successfully. You ... you don't have any social graces ... you're just a pathetic little outcast from America.'

'You stupid bitch,' he shoved her and she fell backwards, tumbling a few steps down the stairs, before she broke the fall with her forearm.

'Owwww, someone help me, please!!!' she shrieked.

Lucidity returned as soon as he saw that she was really hurt. She was holding onto her arm and crying. He was about to help her up but she screamed.

'You bastard! You low-class, no-good bastard! Stay away from me. Stay away!'

So he rushed to his table, grabbed his phone, laptop, T-shirt, and leapt over her crouched body on the stairs and he ran out of the café.

* * *

Later that afternoon Ketut came to his house. Cassandra had suffered some bruises and a badly sprained arm and she would need to use a sling. She was trying to get Pak Agung to press charges against him but all the staff had dissuaded Pak Agung. They said that it was probably just an unfortunate accident because they all knew Mr Mike and they had vouched that he was a good man. So there would not be a police case but Mr Mike had to keep away from the café. In fact it would be better if he gave that whole area a wide berth so that Ibu Cassandra didn't make a big fuss again, Ketut implored.

He walked Ketut to the front gate and they shook hands

solemnly. He stood watching as Ketut walked away. He stood there, still watching, as Ketut disappeared from sight. He stood on that same spot until the tears came, in wave after wave. And he just couldn't stop.

* * *

The sun was touching the horizon now. Soon it would sink out of his sight. The sky was aflame with radiant flashes of copper, vermillion and gold. He was swimming towards the horizon. The sea around him was now a shimmering light-play, reflecting the blazing sky. Each stroke was slower now as his body felt heavier. But he knew nothing was insurmountable. All was possible. The sun was his guide.

monsoonbooks

ISLAND SECRETS

Alwin Blum first set foot ... ine 1990s and has lived in Bali, off and on, for over a decade – for seven of those years, in a small home within a Balinese family compound. The author is an avid student and observer of Balinese culture and healing. Although abysmal at yoga, Blum has been known to meditate from time to time. Blum grew up reading authors like W. Somerset Maugham who wrote about the lives of colonial expats in the tropics and the dark underside of the civilised facade. This collection of stories was inspired by the multitudes from around the world that have flocked to Bali to make it their safe haven.